Life in the Fast Lane

"Duck!" Les shouted. "If my sister sees us, I'm finished!"

Too late. Natalie stopped by the car. When her eyes met Les's, she froze.

"Please!" Les screamed, looking into her incredulous face. "I beg of you! Don't tell Dad! I'll do anything! I promise!"

"Les, what are you doing?" Natalie wailed.

"Just driving." Les shrugged his shoulders.

Oh, please don't say it, Les thought. Not in front of my friends. He could see Dean and Charles staring at Natalie, listening to her every word.

What do you mean, driving?" Natalie continued.

No! Les wanted to scream. DON'T SAY IT!

Natalie put her hands on her hips. And at the top of her lungs, she yelled, "You don't even have a license!"

License to DRIVE

A novelization by A.L. Singer
Based on the motion picture screenplay written
by Neil Tolkin

SCHOLASTIC INC.
New York Toronto London Auckland Sydney

ISBN 0-590-41980-3

12 11 10 9 8 7 6 5   9/8 0 1 2 3/9

Printed in the U.S.A.   01

First Scholastic printing, June 1988

Chapter 1

SCREEEK - SCREEEK - SCREEEK - SCREEEK. . . .

Sweat poured from Les Anderson's brow. Even the smallest muscle in his hand cried out in pain. He looked up, his blue eyes darting wildly back and forth. How could anyone not hear him?

Les quickly scanned the other students on the school bus. Zombies, he thought. That's what they were. Each face was as dull and gray as the clouds that hovered outside. Each pair of eyes stared lifelessly out the grime-caked windows. Not one of them moved a muscle.

Well, maybe *they've* given up, Les said to himself. Maybe *they* don't mind being prisoners in this stinking jail on wheels.

But not me. These chains can't hold Les Anderson.

SCREEEK - SCREEEK - SCREEEK - SCREEEK. . . .

Les worked the file back and forth — patiently, rhythmically. His ankle throbbed from the pressure of the metal shackle. There was just a fraction of an inch left — a fraction of an inch, and he would slice right through the steel lock.

CHINK!

There. Les pulled his foot out of the shackle. Free at last!

Suddenly the bus came to a stop. A red blur flashed outside. Les spun around to see what it was.

As he peered through the layers of grease on the bus window, Les could only tell three crucial things: It was slick. It was shiny. And it *hated* to idle.

He wiped the window clear with his arm and pressed his face against the glass.

And then his jaw dropped open.

He couldn't help it. The sight was enough to stun any sixteen-year-old guy. No, it wasn't so much the sleek, glistening silhouette of the 308 GTS. It wasn't even the deep, rumbling purr of the engine.

It was the legs.

Pure and simple, they were the longest, the smoothest, the sexiest pair of legs Les had ever seen — had ever *imagined* seeing. They lounged in the passenger seat of the Ferrari, in plain sight through the open roof. Les strained to see the face of the girl who owned them.

But it was impossible. Her face was hidden

by the roof. All he could see were her legs and the empty driver's seat. . . .

Empty! Les's eyes lit up. It was almost too good to be true. He looked around. Sure enough, a guy was walking away from the car toward a grocery store.

I'm out of here, Les thought.

He glanced toward the rear exit of the bus. FOR EMERGENCY USE ONLY was marked on it, in huge black letters.

It was his only chance. He perched at the edge of his seat, hoping the bus driver wouldn't notice him.

No such luck. Like laser beams, two beady eyes glared at him in the rearview mirror. Eyes that peered out from beneath a waxy, seedy toupee. Eyes that had the sadistic glint of a true maniac.

A normal person would have shrunk in fear. But not Les. He held the bus driver's stare, strong and unflinching. For a long moment, it looked as if neither of them would move.

Then . . . *ca-chunk.* With a sudden thrust, the driver threw the shift into first gear. The bus pulled away from the Ferrari.

And Les sprang into action. He exploded from his seat, running to the exit. One by one, the heads of the other students began to turn his way. A cheer rang out. It was joined by another cheer. By the time Les was halfway down the aisle, the entire bus had come to life.

Suddenly an alarm pierced the air. Les dove for the door.

Thunk. At that moment, a steel bolt slammed across the door. Les's eyes widened. He was in midair. There was only one thing he could do —

CRAAAASSSSHH! Glass spewed out onto the street as Les flew through the back window. He hit the ground in a perfect commando roll. Hopping to his feet, he sprinted toward the sleek, red car.

With its tires squealing, the school bus skidded into a turnaround — and headed right back toward Les!

But Les's eyes were on the Ferrari. Or to be more exact, on the person *inside* the Ferrari.

Up close, her legs looked even better than they had from the bus. She tossed back her lustrous blonde hair and gazed at Les with the sexiest smile this side of the planet Venus. It was beyond magnetism, beyond electricity. It was a new, savage force that bound the two of them together against the rest of the world.

Les jumped into the car. In his rearview mirror, he could see the bus coming nearer. With swift, sure motions, he switched on the ignition and popped the clutch.

The Ferrari screeched as it took off. Les yanked the steering wheel to the right and headed onto the nearest side street.

The quiet, tree-lined boulevard came to life

with the roar of the car's engine. Within seconds, the bus barreled around the corner, its two left wheels lifting off the ground.

Les glanced at his speedometer: 70 . . . 75 . . . 80 . . . 85. A grin spread across his face — until he looked in the rearview mirror.

He could see nothing but yellow. The yellow of the school bus right on his tail.

Les floored the accelerator. The car shot forward — just as a paperboy pedaled his bicycle onto the street right in front of them! A look of terror shot through the boy's face. Les steered sharply to the left.

He missed the boy by inches . . . but the bus didn't. It sliced off the bike's front tire and sent it flying into the air.

Les breathed a quick sigh of relief. In his mirror, he could see the boy spinning wildly on his rear tire — confused, but alive.

Immediately his eyes shot ahead of him. Between two buildings was a dark, narrow alleyway.

Perfect! Les made an abrupt turn into the alley and glided through. He flashed a triumphant smile. No *chance* the bus would fit through that.

He was wrong. The bus slammed into the alley, smashing against both walls. Sparks shot out from the bus's sides as it pulled down power cables and live wires.

There was still another chance. At the end of the alley was Commercial Boulevard, one of the widest streets in town. Les jammed on the brakes and slid right onto it.

The street stretched out before him like a racetrack. At his side, his luscious partner dangled a cigarette from her slender fingers. With one hand, Les downshifted to accelerate. With the other, he reached out to light the cigarette.

And as she gently pulled Les's hand toward her, the Ferrari took off like a long, red streak of light. Les's lips spread into a confident grin.

But the danger was not over. Not by a long shot. In front of them, Les could make out something very slick and shiny on the road. It looked like a water spill. But he wasn't quite close enough to tell. . . .

Just then his eyes popped wide open. Next to the road, a huge fuel truck was being gassed up. A clear liquid spray was spewing out onto the street from a ruptured hose. Les was streaking right toward a shimmering pool of gasoline!

At that moment, a hazy, monotonous voice popped into his head:

" . . . *Remember,*" the voice droned. *"Be prepared and look ahead. The driver must see the big picture. In heavier rain, your tires may begin to 'hydroplane' — ride on the water instead of the pavement. Don't panic! And especially don't jam on the brakes. Ease your foot off the gas pedal. . . ."*

Images flashed through Les's head: a

film projector, driver's ed books, falling asleep. . . .

Les raced toward the gas spill. There was no way to avoid it. Obeying the voice in his head, he lifted his foot off the gas pedal.

The Ferrari plunged through. A tidal wave of gas sprayed up into the air on either side.

As they came roaring out, Les laughed nonchalantly. The girl looked at him with admiring eyes as he reached over to finish lighting her cigarette.

Then, with a casual but knowing flick of the wrist, he tossed the still-lit match out the window.

BAAAAA-ROOOOOOOOOM! The Ferrari shook. The ground underneath it shook. Les jammed on the brakes. He and the girl turned around to see a wall of bright orange flames consume the road behind them. The school bus was history.

Les raised an eyebrow. With his best, most modest Tom Cruise smile, he looked at the girl. Already her lips were parted. Already she was staring at him with a look that said, Les, I'm yours. Now and forever.

It must be destiny, Les thought, as he brought his lips closer to hers. His eyelids slowly shut.

But not before he saw her mouth fall open in shock. Les pulled back. He followed her bug-eyed stare out the back window.

In the next split second, his entire life passed before him — just the highlights:

birth, discovery of TV, getting out of grammar school. There wasn't time for anything else. Hurtling toward them was a terrifying sight — the mangled, hulking, metal grill of the school bus, inches away from collision!

Chapter 2

BRRRRIIIIIIIING!

Les yanked his head up. His eyes popped open. He let out an involuntary gasp. The school bus! Where was it?

A drop of cold sweat fell into his eye. For a second, everything was blurry. He blinked.

When all was clear, he looked up — and found himself staring into the face of the bus driver!

But it wasn't the bus driver, really. It was . . . it was his teacher, Mr. Gasket!

Les's mind was beginning to clear. He knew exactly where he was now. He could feel his face turning red with embarrassment. In the back of the room, a movie projector was rewinding. In the front, a list had been scrawled on the blackboard, under the heading *DRIVER'S ED: RULES OF THE ROAD.*

Les's twin sister Natalie walked toward the classroom door with her friend Roxanne.

Both girls looked at Les and shook their heads.

"Does your brother have mono or something?" Roxanne asked with a sneer. "He slept through the entire course."

"No, he's just brain-dead," Natalie answered. With that, the two girls stepped through the door.

That left just two people in the classroom — Les and Mr. Gasket. Les sank into his seat as the teacher strode toward him.

Mr. Gasket had taught driver's ed since before Les was born. No one in Sunny Meadows High could get a license without passing his course. It was said he held the job because he *enjoyed* watching students fail at something they wanted so badly. Rumor had it that some of his students were still trying to get their licenses — at age thirty!

Another rumor had it that he used motor oil to keep up the sheen on his toupee.

Mr. Gasket loomed above Les, his hairpiece gleaming in the reflected light from the ceiling. "Mr. Anderson," he said, "it's punks like you the paramedics end up scraping off the roads at four in the morning." He leaned over the desk, looking down his crooked nose. "For your own sake and the safety of others, I hope you fail your driver's exam."

Les got up from his seat, but Mr. Gasket held out his left hand, signaling him to stay.

With his right hand, he threw Les a piece of chalk and pointed to the blackboard.

And Les felt his stomach sink as he realized there was no way he'd catch the early bus.

The sounds of laughter and bus engines filtered in through the open classroom window.

I WILL DRIVE SAFELY.

That's one hundred seventy-five, Les said to himself. He shook out his cramped, chalk-covered fingers and kept on writing.

"Only twenty-five more," Mr. Gasket said, staring out the window. "But you'd better hurry if you want to make the late bus."

I WILL DRIVE SAFELY. I WILL DRIVE SAFELY.

One hundred seventy-six. One hundred seventy-seven. . . . Les's fingers raced across the blackboard. Just wait till I get my license, Les thought. Just wait, Mr. Gasket. I won't be a slave to any bus schedule. When I blow out of here, it'll be on my own time. And I'll send a blast of exhaust through this window that'll blow that greasy rug right off your head.

I WILL DRIVE SAFELY.

Two hundred! Before the chalk could clatter to the metal holder, Les was out of the classroom.

He raced to his locker and yanked it open, bringing an avalanche of books, pencils, candy wrappers, and soda cans down on his head. He stuffed them back in and slammed the locker shut.

He bombed through the hallway, stuffing papers into his knapsack. And as he reached the front door, the bus pulled away from the curb.

Les's white Nikes pounded the pavement as he ran. But it was too little, too late. The bus sped down the street, shifting into third gear. Through the rear window, he could see the gloating face of his sister Natalie.

He stopped in the middle of the road, fuming. He felt so . . . so . . . *powerless*. That was the word. It was more than embarrassment, more than anger. Without a driver's license, his life was *nothing*. What girl would look at a guy who had to run after a school bus? How far could a guy get with a girl, knowing that his mother would be by to pick him up at 10:00, because she needed to get to bed by 10:45? Les punched the air in frustration. High school life was a *nightmare*. It rewarded nerds like Natalie, who did everything by the book and didn't care about the finer things in life. Like roaring along the highway at a cool 80 mph, like busting out of the garage like a fuel-injected animal sprung from a cage, like showing up at your fourth party of the night at 1 A.M. with the hottest-looking girl in the class.

Lost in his thoughts, Les was only vaguely

aware of the car engine behind him. It got louder and louder and louder. . . .

Les snapped out of his funk. He wheeled around to see a red streak heading right for him — the red streak of a speeding Ferrari 308 GTS. He jumped out of the way as it screamed by him, but his eyes caught sight of the two passengers. The driver looked like he had just stepped out of the pages of the magazine *GQ*. Paolo was his name, Les remembered. Paolo, the luckiest man in Sunny Meadows, the man who could claim Mercedes Lane as his girlfriend.

Les could see tufts of Mercedes's blonde hair flicker out through the open roof. She was sitting in the passenger seat, exactly as he'd imagined her in his dream. . . .

EEEEEEEEEEEEEEEEEE! Instinctively Les whipped his head around to see a bike sliding along at the end of a thirty-foot-long skid mark — and stopping one inch before his foot.

But Les didn't move a muscle. It was only Dean. Car-obsessed, girl-obsessed Dean, whose bike was more a weapon than a vehicle. Dean was Les's best friend, and maybe the only person in the world who wanted a license more than Les did.

Together they watched the Ferrari disappear into the distance. Les sighed. "You know, Dean, I can't help wondering whether it'll ever get that good for me."

Dean narrowed his dark brown eyes. "Anderson, the only difference between you and that jerk is that he has a license and you don't. In two days we open a whole new chapter!" He motioned to his handlebars. "Get in. I'll drive you home."

Les's lips couldn't help but curl up with disdain. Dean's bike looked as if someone had thrown it in a swamp, taken it out, left it in the rain to rust, and then jumped on top of it.

"Unh-uh," Les answered, shaking his head. "Too much is at stake. They'll never let me take my driver's exam in traction."

Dean cocked his head and put on a sincere expression. "Les, your license is as important to me as it is to you. I'll take it easy. I promise."

"Yeeeeeeee-haaahhh!"

Dean yelled at the top of his lungs, as he weaved in and out of traffic. His short, lank brown hair was pushed straight back by the wind. Les felt the bones in his spine crunch together as Dean jolted the bike off the street and onto the sidewalk.

Dean zigzagged onto a side street, sending a jogger hurtling out of the way. He threw his head back with laughter.

Thwack! Les couldn't duck away as Dean pedaled through low-hanging branches. He sat back up, his face stinging — just in time to see the razor-sharp teeth of a huge angry dog, inches from his ankle!

At the last minute, with a wild whoop, Dean swerved away. The dog lurched into the air, pulled back by his tether.

Les's fingers were white from clutching onto the handlebars. His jaw ached from clenching his teeth in fear. Finally his house came into view. His friendly, welcoming house with its perfectly groomed lawn, macadam driveway — and sprinkler!

Foooosh! Dean's bike made wet marks on the driveway as he drove right under the cascade of water, sending a cold shock right through Les.

In front of the garage was the Audi 5000 Turbo that belonged to Les's mom. Around it were mounds of dusty boxes, tools, and garden equipment. Dean plowed right through, sending the stuff flying. Just a few feet in front of them, nestled peacefully in the garage, was the back of a gleaming, mint-condition '72 Cadillac Sedan De Ville.

Dean jammed on the brakes. Les closed his eyes. The tires shrieked as the bike stopped inches from the bumper.

It's over, Les said to himself as he opened his eyes and slid off the handlebars, his body contorted with pain. He turned to give Dean a withering look.

"Just a painful reminder of what you're leaving behind," Dean said with a smirk. Then he nodded in the direction of the car. "Whose Caddy?"

"My grandfather's," Les replied, stretching himself out. "Can you believe it has only twenty thousand miles on it?"

Dean hopped off his bike and let it crash to the ground. "It's intense. What's it doing here?"

"He's afraid to take it on long trips so he borrowed my dad's car for a week."

Dean ran his fingers along the chrome trim and opened the door. "I tell you, Les, this boat would knock 'em dead up at Archie's. Do you think we can get it for Saturday night?"

From behind them, a low-pitched voice boomed, "Not a chance, Dean."

Les and Dean turned to see Mr. Anderson ambling toward them. His dark mustache had a layer of dust on it, and his work clothes looked as if they were dying to jump into a washing machine. With a flick of his hand, he removed Dean's hand from the car. Then he buffed the chrome with a rag. "You have a better chance of winning the Nobel Prize in physics," he continued, glowering at Dean. "Now, how about a hand helping me move this junk?"

Dean and Les surveyed the boxes and equipment strewn all over the driveway.

Immediately Dean coughed. He leaned down to pick up his bike. "I'd really love to, Mr. Anderson, but I'm sort of allergic to dust and cardboard boxes." He hopped on the bike, coughing again. "See you tonight."

Les watched as Dean disappeared down the driveway. After I get my license Saturday,

I will never, *never* have to ride on that thing again, he thought. A smile crept across his face. I'll come straight home, throw my license on the table for all to see, get dressed, and then cut out of here —

Suddenly Les realized he was making a big assumption. He looked at his dad, who was shuffling among the boxes. Was this a good time to bring up a sore subject? Oh well, there was no harm in trying.

"Um, Dad? Do you think you could tell me for sure if I can use Mom's car Saturday night?"

Say yes, Les wanted to scream out. Or nod your head, or just grunt if you're too busy. I mean, we all know I'll be legal by Saturday — and this party could make my reputation. I just need you to give me the word.

Les's father stood up, a dusty box in his arms. He looked his son squarely in the eye. There was a tense moment of silence. Then he shoved the box into Les's chest. "Do me a favor, will you, Les? Just pass your driver's exam. Then we'll talk."

Chapter 3

Yechhhh!

Les felt his stomach turn. He wanted to run away from the dinner table, or at least *say* something. But he sat still, reminding himself over and over: She's pregnant, she's pregnant, she's pregnant.

Les's mom walked toward the table, carrying the last steaming plate of food. For nine months Les had watched her abdomen grow. For nine months he had seen her taste get more and more bizarre. But nothing had prepared him for this.

Not that he had anything against mashed potatoes. He *loved* mashed potatoes, and there were plenty on the plate for the whole family. Of course, their plates were already full, but that didn't matter. He didn't even mind the fact that the plate was rimmed with potato chips — that seemed like an interesting idea.

Maybe it was the wet, slimy pickles she'd dumped on top. Or the chocolate chips. . . .

Les could see his dad, Natalie, and his ten-year-old brother Rudy all looking at her in disbelief. Even Rudy couldn't stomach this — and he could eat *anything*! Les grabbed for his spoon and hoped he could find some area of the potatoes where the pickle brine hadn't soaked through.

But instead of putting the plate in the middle of the table, Mrs. Anderson plopped it right down at her place setting.

And as everyone's eyes bulged in disgust, she picked up a bottle of ketchup and began squirting it all over the concoction.

Mrs. Anderson looked up. She returned her family's stares with a placid grin, her blue eyes twinkling beneath a shock of curly red hair. "For your information," she said, "this is exactly what I ate when I was pregnant with all of you."

As she opened her mouth to take a first bite, they all quickly averted their eyes downward and dug into their own meals.

Les played with his food for a second, then turned to his dad. "Dad?"

"Mm-hmm?" Mr. Anderson replied, with a mouthful of food.

"Did you get a chance to look at those brochures?"

Mr. Anderson pulled a crumpled-up pamphlet out of his back pocket. The letters

BMW were emblazoned across the front of it. "Sure did."

Why did he always have to look so *blank*? Les could never tell what he was feeling. Wait — was that a smile beginning to form on his face as he flipped through the brochure? Les's heart began to race.

"A twenty-three-thousand-dollar car for a sixteen-year-old kid who's never had a job in his life?" Mr. Anderson said flatly. "I think it's a great idea."

Les let out a frustrated sigh and looked glumly at his plate.

"Les, you only completed your driver's ed course two hours ago," his father continued. "You don't even have a license yet."

"But Dad," Les replied, "it wouldn't just be for me. It would be for Natalie, too!"

Natalie gave him a scornful glare. "Don't include *me* in your obsession."

"Well, excuuuuse me, Miss Mature!" Les retorted. "Is there anything wrong with being American?"

"A BMW at sixteen?" Natalie said. "It's more like *spoiled*. Karl says — "

Everyone dropped their forks and leaned toward her, as if waiting for a divine message from on high.

Natalie rolled her eyes. "Can't you people please be serious for once in your life?" She lifted her chin and went on. "Karl says that in America the people are misled to believe that a car represents freedom and individuality. In essence, it is more oppressive than anything else, burdening the individual with materialistic costs, such as insurance, gas, and repairs."

"Who cares what your boyfriend thinks?" Les shot back. "He should sell his car and move to Russia if he's so concerned about materialism!"

"I agree," Rudy piped up.

"You two are so simple it's frightening," Natalie said.

"Why are you even getting your license, Natalie?" Les taunted.

Natalie's face clouded over. She pushed her chair back from the table and got up. "I'm not hungry."

Les's mom shot a stern look at Natalie. "I've had just about enough of this silly arguing. Natalie, if you prefer to eat standing up, that's fine with me. But nobody leaves the table until we finish eating."

"This is the most oppressive environment a child could be subjected to," Natalie replied. She folded her arms and sat down.

HONNNNK! The blast of a car horn made everyone jump.

Instantly Les shot up out of his seat. "That's for me!" he said, wiping his mouth.

"You heard me, Les," Mrs. Anderson said. "Whoever it is will have to wait a few minutes."

Les fidgeted impatiently, refusing to sit. "But *Maaaaa —* "

"Les?" Mrs. Anderson continued. "Do you want to use my car Saturday night?"

That did it. Les dropped into his chair as if it had a pants-magnet. He quickly put a forkful of vegetables in his mouth.

HONNNNK! HONNNNK!

Natalie's eyes shifted to Les, then to Mrs. Anderson. She twirled her fork on her plate.

HONK-HONK!

Rudy made a face and looked around the table. The horn was making everyone edgy — except Les. With a peaceful smile, he cheerfully munched away.

HONNNNNNNNNNNNNNNNNNNNNK!

Dad's fork clattered to the plate. His face did a slow burn. "Les," he said with a measured tone, "if you're not out of this house in five seconds, there's a good chance you'll never drive anything but a golf ball."

Les grinned. "Excuse me."

He calmly rose from the table, put down his napkin, and bolted toward the front door.

Outside, a rusted Datsun B-210 awaited. Dean was in the backseat, stretching over to the front and pressing on the horn. In the front seat, Dean's mother and little sister leaned away from him, with dull resignation. They were used to this.

Les ran to the back door of the Datsun and threw it open. For a split second, he stopped and stared. There was so little room between the back and front seat, he could barely see the carpet. He squeezed in as

Dean wiggled down at his end. Dean's little sister turned around and grinned. There was enough room between her and the dashboard to fit a pinball machine.

As the car inched away from the curb, Les's and Dean's knees were practically in their throats. Never again, Les vowed to himself. From Saturday on, whenever I go somewhere, it's in the driver's seat.

If he ever got to Saturday. The way his body was contorted, one wrong move and he would be asphyxiated.

All he could do for now was sit tight and pray they didn't go over any bumps.

Chapter 4

"Ahhhh-haaaa! Hey, boys, does Mommy drive you to the little boys' room, too?"

Les cringed as he got out of the car. Dean had told his mom to drop them off around the corner from the party. It was essential to their entrance. On a quiet side street, no one would see them being driven by a *mother*, with a *sister* tagging along, in a beat-up old *jalopy*.

Or so they thought.

If they could have chosen the worst people to see them, it would have been the three jerks in the primer gray GTO across the street. As the car slowed down, Les couldn't help getting a glimpse of their faces.

And the sight wasn't pretty. All three of them looked as if they'd dropped out of high school sometime in the previous decade — and taken a bath maybe three times since. Their beard stubble could probably file glass into powder — which made sense, because that's probably what they ate for breakfast. The three goons howled with laughter, pointing at Les and Dean as they drove away. The Jolly Roger on their antenna flapped in the breeze, and their car horn blared out the tune of a funeral march.

Dean leaned back toward the Datsun. "Sorry I didn't introduce you, Ma," he said dryly. "See you at twelve."

"I'll be right here at eleven," came the answer.

"I'll call," Dean said.

"It's a school night, Dean," she said firmly. "If you're not standing here between eleven and eleven-oh-two, I'm changing the locks."

Before Dean could say another word, the Datsun took off down the street.

Dean straightened out his shirt. He gave Les a shrug, and the two of them sauntered toward the party. As they got close, the pounding beat of the music practically shook the sidewalk. In Les's neighborhood, someone would have called the cops by now. But here, it probably didn't matter, Les thought. The houses — no, *mansions* — were so far apart that no one would notice.

They turned the corner into a winding driveway — and instantly Les's eyes lit up. There, huddled around polished, glittery driving machines, were the most drop-dead gorgeous girls in the area — maybe in the world. It never failed, the girls who looked like a

million bucks during the day look like . . .
like the *national deficit* at night.

No, that didn't sound right . . . ah, what
was the difference? Les thought. They were
all out of reach, anyway — for now. Looking
around the party, the pecking order became
clear. It wasn't necessarily the best-looking
guys who had the cutest girls, or the biggest
guys, or even the coolest. It was the guys
who had the slickest cars.

Let's face it, Les said to himself, I'm at
the bottom of the ladder here. No, without
a license, I'm *below* the ladder. I'm the mound
of dirt.

Just then his thoughts were interrupted
by the slamming of a car door. Just ahead
of them, a familiar teenaged guy with glasses
cheerfully waved good-bye as his mother
pulled away in a Honda — directly in front
of the mansion, in full sight of everyone at
the party.

"I don't believe this," Les groaned.

"I do," Dean said. "It's vintage Charles.
Ignorance is bliss."

Suddenly the guy with glasses saw them.
"Les! Dean!" he called out, waving with even
more enthusiasm.

"Eyes left!" Dean commanded, and he and
Les walked into the party without stopping
for a second.

From the mansion itself to the street, the
party was practically exploding with activity.

Girls danced in outfits that looked as if they'd been painted on — by someone who wanted to spare as much paint as possible. And judging from the looks of the guys, the stock of every styling-mousse company must have risen to new heights that week. Caterers raced in and out of the mansion, and the sound of clattering plates and silverware rang out from the kitchen.

In fact, there was only one area of the estate that was quiet, one area that had been ignored by most of the crowd — the front steps. That was the private domain of Les, Dean, and Charles.

All alone, the three of them sipped fruit punch and surveyed the scene. Their wide eyes flitted from car to car, where girls seemed to outnumber guys three to one.

"I know exactly what you're thinking, Les. I'm thinking the same thing." Dean cast a quick glance at Charles, who was bouncing blissfully to the music. "Of course, I can't speak for Charles. . . ."

Charles frowned at him, but Dean just plowed on. "Why am I so alone here? I'm good-looking, I've got a great sense of humor, and yet there's not one single female within twenty yards of me! Can you find *one* of them who isn't within arm's reach of a car?"

Les nodded sadly. "They've even monopolized the fifteen-year-old girls."

"You know, you guys are pathetic,"

Charles said, rolling his eyes. "Life *does* exist outside a V-Eight."

"Not in this country, it doesn't," Les answered.

"And do you know what the beauty of it all is?" Dean added. "The beauty of it all, Les, is that Saturday afternoon, less than forty-eight hours away, the people at the DMV are going to be handing you your license . . . our future!"

Our future. The words had a magic ring. Les's mood was beginning to lift.

"You can say good-bye to the humiliation of public transportation, and not being able to date someone who isn't conveniently close to a bus stop," Dean went on. "You're going to be free, Les. One of *them*."

Les caught sight of a guy leaning up against a Lamborghini. Beneath the guy's sunglasses, his lips inched upward into the tiniest, slightest smile. Immediately four incredibly beautiful girls around him started laughing. Les put himself in the guy's place. He felt his spirits start to soar.

Dean's voice rose in intensity. "And on Saturday night, when we pull into Archie's Atomic Broiler in your mom's Audi 5000 Turbo, all this is going to be at our fingertips. In fact, Archie's makes this place look like *Sesame Street*."

"To you, Archie's makes *Miami Vice* look like *Sesame Street*," Charles muttered.

Dean ignored the remark. "My brother

used to go there every weekend," he said. "He says the ratio of girls to guys is five to one. And we're not talking *dogs*, we're talking *bunnies*. The place is a paradise! I'm telling you, Les. The secret to your happiness, and ultimately *our* happiness, is a driver's license!"

"You can't possibly believe that garbage, can you?" said Charles.

Dean looked out at the swarm of people surrounding the cars. "Charles, seeing is believing."

Charles fell silent. There really was no arguing that point.

Dean took a last swig of his punch and stood up. "All this leering is sapping my energy. I'm going inside to get some more punch."

Les and Charles followed him into the softly lit living room of the mansion. Music echoed off the walls and mixed with the din of laughter and talking. Students milled around the punchbowl, danced on the floor, necked on the couches and armchairs. None of them seemed to notice Les, Dean, and Charles as they moved through the crowd.

Les slumped over the punchbowl, looking around him with envy.

"If you found yourself in the backseat of a car with one of these wenches, do you ever wonder what kind of car it would be?" Dean asked.

"You never cease to amaze me, Deano," Charles said.

"Seriously," Dean insisted. "Look at Cheryl Lieberman."

Les looked over at a girl with heavy makeup and dark fingernails, which she kept staring at, as if she were afraid they'd fall off.

"A Camaro?" Charles guessed.

"Cheryl Lieberman? A Trans Am," Les said.

Dean looked over at a pristine-looking blonde, dressed in the most conservative clothes this side of L. L. Bean. "Beth Maclaine."

"A Volvo," Les suggested. "Maybe a station wagon."

"Bonnie Dupa," Dean said.

Charles and Dean turned to see the face of a girl dressed in wild clothes with garish makeup, chomping on gum.

"A van," Charles said, getting into the spirit.

"Nah, a Harley," Dean said.

But Les's eyes were caught by someone else, someone absolutely exquisite. The only word out of his mouth was a hushed "Mercedes."

Dean and Charles both spun around to him and said in disbelief, "A Mercedes?"

Les wasn't listening. He was only vaguely aware that his mouth was hanging open, that his eyes were popping out of his head. Standing in the doorway, her long legs silhouetted through her dress by the light behind her, was a figure so sultry and smoldering that Les thought he would burn up just from looking.

"Mercedes Lane," he murmured.

Dean and Charles couldn't help matching Les, gawk for gawk. "What more can be said?" Dean whispered in awe.

"I've bumped into her a million times, and she's never once bumped into me," Les said.

Suddenly Mercedes stormed away from the doorway, directly toward them. Her stiletto heels dug holes in the carpet. Behind her was Paolo, looking about five years older than everyone else — and very uncomfortable.

Mercedes's voice rose above the noise. "You don't own me," she yelled to Paolo. "I can do whatever I like. Women have rights, you know. I don't care if you're used to women worshipping the ground you walk on!"

She barged through Les, Dean, and Charles as if they weren't there. Les stepped away, but she stopped right beside him and poured herself some punch. He felt his body begin to quiver. Steady, Les, he said to himself. Enjoy it. This may be the most exciting moment of your life.

"It has nothing to do with worship," Paolo pleaded, looking around him uneasily. "It has to do with going to parties with . . . with kids!"

"I happen to go to school with these kids," Mercedes snapped. "I have friends here."

"Friends?" Paolo retorted. "These *children* can do nothing for you."

With an icy edge to her voice, Mercedes said, "Can we just stop this discussion? There are some things you and I will never agree on."

"Mercedes," Paolo said, flustered. "I'm beginning to perspire. You know I hate to perspire." He turned on his heels to go, then looked back over his shoulder. "Are you coming?"

"I think I can find my way, thank you," Mercedes replied.

Paolo turned his back to her and strutted toward the door.

"And Paolo?" Mercedes said, seething. "If you're wondering about Saturday night, I just remembered — "

Paolo whipped back around. "Don't do this to me, Mercedes. You'll regret it."

"I've made other plans," Mercedes went on. "I have a date."

"With who?"

"With . . . *him!*" Mercedes spun around and pointed at the first person she saw.

Les.

Chapter 5

At that moment, Les felt as though he'd been paid a visit by Santa Claus, Hugh Hefner, and Darth Vader.

Paolo's eyes widened in shock. *"Him?"*

Mercedes looked furiously at Les. "Didn't we make arrangements?"

"I — I believe so," Les stammered. He felt Paolo's eyes burning a hole in him. "But, uh, nothing was final."

"Well, now they're final," Mercedes said.

Paolo's mouth was tight from forcing back anger. "You'll pay for this, Mercedes," he said through clenched teeth. With that, he stormed away.

Mercedes lifted her glass to her lips and belted down the punch. A bitter smile creased her otherwise perfect face, and she turned away from Les as if he'd never been there.

But Les didn't even notice. It was all he could do to keep himself from floating off the ground.

* * *

"I cannot believe you," Dean said the next day as he climbed into the bus behind Charles. He paused on the steps and turned around to look at Les, who was still on the sidewalk. "You're about to blow the greatest night of your life for a girl who doesn't know you have a pulse! After all these years, we finally get a chance to go to Archie's, and now you're telling me it's off?"

"If Mercedes pulls through, you bet," Les replied.

Charles leaned over Dean's shoulder and said, "Why don't you ask her, to make sure?"

Les shrugged. "I'd love to, Charles. But I can't talk to something I can't see. Last night was the closest any of us have ever been to her."

Dean looked over his shoulder and smirked. "Well, you're in luck, Lover boy, 'cause she's sitting down right behind you."

He stepped up into the bus, smiling — and the doors slammed in Les's face.

Trapped.

Les turned around. A few feet away, Mercedes sat on a bench, reading a glossy fashion magazine and sipping apple juice. As the bus drove off, Les walked timidly toward her. Her soft blonde hair glinted like spun gold as it fluttered in the wind. He watched her every move, memorizing each gesture — the way her hand turned the page, the way her mouth closed around the straw.

A drop of apple juice dribbled on her lower lip. She licked it off with a languid sweep of her tongue. Les fought to keep his knees from buckling.

Now he was inches away from her. Her eyes flickered up at him briefly.

Not a trace of recognition.

Then . . . *HONNNNK! HONNNNK!* "Les!" a familiar voice called out.

Les jumped. Of all the times for his *father* to drive by — in that huge turquoise *boat* of a car, with a horn that sounded like an out-of-tune brass band!

Pulling himself together, Les strolled past Mercedes as if absolutely nothing had happened. Then he nonchalantly walked across the street, right in front of the Caddy.

"Les, it's me! Your father!"

Les wanted to crawl into a hole. He skulked along the other side of the street, then turned the corner.

Les's dad followed him. When they were finally out of Mercedes's sight, Les went over to the car.

"What's going on here, Les? Didn't you recognize me?" his father said impatiently.

Les opened the door and got in. He noticed an enormous box of paper diapers and a bag of groceries in the backseat. "Dad, what are you doing here?"

"I ran some errands for your mom and I thought I'd come by to take you driving. I figured if you could handle this cruiser you could handle anything." He shrugged. "Grandpa's got *my* car. Who knows what he's doing with it?"

Les felt a grin spread across his face. "Okay," he said, his voice tinged with excitement.

He changed seats with his father and began driving slowly through the neighborhood, stopping short at stop signs, making turns a little too sharply.

But it didn't take him too long to get the hang of it. As he pulled up smoothly at a stop sign, Mr. Anderson nodded with approval. "Not bad," he said.

Suddenly Les froze. He felt his hands gripping the steering wheel, his foot locking on the brake.

"That's a long enough stop," Mr. Anderson said. "Make a right here."

"I . . . I can't," Les said, his eyes focused straight ahead. Slinking down the sidewalk, just ahead of them, was Mercedes.

"What's the matter?"

"Dad, I have to ask you a favor. You see that girl up ahead? Her name is Mercedes Lane. To put it simply, if she asked me to marry her tomorrow, I'd definitely say yes."

Mr. Anderson's eyes sparkled. "So let's drive by her."

"Dad, she just asked me out last night. If I drive by with you in the car, she'll never look at me again."

There was a short silence. Mr. Anderson's

expression turned to disbelief. "You're asking me to let you drive this car, alone? Without a license? Are you insane?"

"I'll just drive by, say hello, and circle back," Les promised. "It'll take two minutes. I . . . I just want to see if she was serious."

Mr. Anderson looked deeply into his son's pleading eyes. Then he glanced up at Mercedes, who was now a block away. The sight of her seemed to make his will soften.

After all, he was human. And male.

Finally he smiled at Les and said, "Sure."

"And Dad . . . " Les said, looking at the huge diaper box in the backseat. "Would you mind?"

Resigned, Mr. Anderson grabbed the box and the grocery bag, and got out of the car. As Les pulled away, he gave his dad a quick wave.

Seconds later he cruised by Mercedes and pressed the car horn.

HONNNK!

Mercedes threw him a nasty glance and kept on walking.

"Mercedes?" Les called out. She stopped and looked inside the car, puzzled. "Les Anderson," he reminded her, "from the party last night."

"Oh, you scared me," Mercedes replied. "I didn't recognize you. Some jerk honked at me a little while ago in a car just like this."

"You live around here, don't you?"

"Uh-huh. Just up the street."

"Hop in, I'll give you a lift."

"Sure, that'd be fun."

As she reached for the front door on the passenger side, Les said, "Wait a second!"

He ran around to her side and pulled open the rear door as if he were a chauffeur.

With a smile that made the noonday sun look dull, she stepped in.

Les went back around to his side, hopped in, and adjusted his rearview mirror. He smiled at the reflection of Mercedes's face and drove off.

"Which house is yours?" he asked.

"It's right down the block." She leaned forward and pointed. "That one over there. . . ."

"Okay," Les said, and smoothly turned into the driveway. What a piece of cake this was!

"But I'm not going home," Mercedes said.

Les stepped on the brake. "Uh . . . where are you going?"

"Into Cedarwood, to a friend's place. You don't mind, do you?"

Les tried to conceal a frightened gulp. In his mirror, he could see the distant, forlorn image of his father, holding the box of diapers. What was he supposed to do now? If he took Mercedes, his dad would *kill* him — but if he didn't, he'd never have a chance with her again. . . .

His hands shaking, he pulled back onto the road. And in a choked, weakened voice, he said, "No, not at all."

Chapter 6

"This is it," Mercedes said, pointing up the road to an enormous estate. Les pulled up to it and she hopped out the door. "Thanks a lot. Now, you know how to get back, right?"

Les nodded with self-assurance. He looked around. Absolutely nothing was familiar. All the homes in the neighborhood were set back on rolling lawns, behind rows of palms and juniper trees. The roads wound up and down mysterious, steep canyons.

But none of that mattered. Not when the most important question of Les's life was burning in his brain.

" 'Bye!" Mercedes said, turning toward the estate.

"Mercedes?" Les called after her.

She turned around. "Uh-huh?"

Okay, Les, it's do or die, he said to himself. You've just put your life on the line, you don't know if you'll ever be welcome in your own house again . . . if you can't do it now, you'll never do it.

"Last night at the party . . . you mentioned something about you and I going out Saturday night. I was just curious — are we still on?"

Mercedes smiled at him. Les thought he detected a trace of pity behind the smile — but it *was* a smile. An honest-to-goodness smile from the most luscious creation in this hemisphere.

"Sure," she said. "Call me tomorrow."

Les pulled a pen out of his pocket. "Great, let me give you my number in case something comes up. You never know."

Les barely remembered writing his number on the cover of her fashion magazine. And he *definitely* had no idea how he found his way out of Cedarwood. In fact, his head was somewhere above the nearest cumulus cloud until he was in Sunny Meadows — two and a half blocks from his own house, to be exact.

That's when the sight of a smoldering, sweaty man caused reality to come crashing in — a man lugging a box of diapers, who happened to be his father.

Les swallowed and looked up from the living room chair. If he had ever wondered what it felt like to be circled by a shark, he knew now.

"How could you do it, Les?" Mr. Anderson said, pacing slowly around him. "You gave me your word *and* you used up your last favor. Do you realize where this leaves you?"

"Not in good shape," Les replied, "but let me explain! I admit I should never have let her in the car — but she lived three houses down. I thought I was taking her home."

It isn't working, Les thought — Dad was too angry to listen. But there was always *Mom*. She would understand a chivalrous act. The sound of her pregnancy-workout video blared in from the den. He could see her doing a scissors-kick exercise — or trying to. "Mom," he called out, "I'm sure there were many similar romantic gestures when Dad was dating you."

Mrs. Anderson paused and thought for a second. "I don't know," she said with a smile. "There must have been — we're married."

Exasperation flashed across Mr. Anderson's face. He shot his wife a glance, then turned back to Les. "Why didn't you just tell her the truth?"

"Tell Mercedes Lane I don't have a license? And risk her having a heart attack from laughing so much?" Les gave his dad a meaningful, man-to-man look. "Put yourself in my shoes."

That seemed to do the trick. His dad pulled back, flustered. He looked at his wife for support, but she just smiled and shrugged.

With a nod of his head, he admitted defeat. "Well," he said, "consider yourself lucky *I* didn't have a heart attack walking home."

* * *

With slow precision, Les carefully maneuvered his scissors around Mercedes's yearbook picture. For all he cared, Dean and Charles could have been miles away, instead of in his room. Any other time he would have hated to see Charles pawing through his CD collection, Dean drumming on his TV set, or worse, hear that horrendous classical music seeping in through the bedroom wall from Natalie's room.

But when Mercedes was involved, everything else just seemed to fade into the background.

"Do you know what happens if you get caught driving without a license?" Dean said, agitated. "They make you wait *two years* before you can take the test again. Twenty-four months, Les. That's a lot of bus rides."

"Relax. I didn't get caught. Besides, you'd do the same," Les said. He picked up the picture of Mercedes and pinned it over his desk. "Now, did you guys come over here to ask me some questions or what?"

Les picked up his driver's manual and held it out toward his friends. A tense silence hung in the air. The classical music began getting louder.

Dean threw up his hands impatiently. "This is a complete waste of time. You know your stuff, Les. You've been a passenger in a car for sixteen years. It's not like you're from *Bedrock* or some — "

A crashing chord of piano and string instruments boomed through the walls.

"What *is* that noise?" Dean asked. He jumped onto Les's bed and reached for an electronic gadget on the night table.

On the other side of the wall, Natalie sat at her desk swaying to the strains of a Tchaikovsky concerto. At the same time, she ran her fingers along a line in her driver's manual and jotted down a note on a piece of paper. Closing her eyes, she tried to memorize the rule about No Standing Zones. But the music was taking over her consciousness, lifting her out of the mundane world of automobiles. She rose from her seat, transported by the passionate chords. She felt her soul being liberated, transported to nineteenth-century Russia, to a romantic snow-covered cottage in the Ural Mountains . . . a roaring fireplace, heated philosophical discussions over vodka . . . paradise. . . .

"Hey, *Naaaaaaataleeeee*!"

Natalie jumped back with a start. The shrill, nasal sound over the intercom was more like a bleat than a voice. Her eyes began to fill with rage. How *humiliating* to be brought back to earth by that . . . that materialistic, automobile-crazed monster —

"If you were in a car traveling at the speed of fifty-five miles per hour and you collided with a runaway train, would that create any improvement in your face?" Dean's voice blared. And then . . . "*BRRRRRRRUUUP!*"

The pencil in Natalie's hand snapped. A

burp, she thought. This is how these intellectual firebrands amuse themselves.

A gale of laughter sounded in the background, as Dean called out, "Good luck on your exam tomorrow, Einstein!"

Natalie fumed inside. We'll see who has the last laugh after that exam, she thought.

Les chuckled as he read the computer screen at the Department of Motor Vehicles:

1. WHAT SHOULD YOU DO IF YOU MISS YOUR EXIT FROM THE EXPRESSWAY?
    A. JAM ON THE BRAKES AND BACK UP.
    B. MAKE A QUICK U-TURN.
    C. GO ON TO THE NEXT EXIT.

Confidently he pressed C.

CORRECT, the screen glowed. Les smiled.

The next question had a sketch of three traffic lanes: lane A was the left, lane B the middle, and lane C the right.

2. WHICH IS THE SMOOTHEST LANE OF TRAFFIC?

"Why don't they just *give* licenses away?" Les murmured to himself. He pressed C.

WRONG.

"*What?*" Les said aloud. He stared at the terminal in shock. Out of the corner of his eye he caught a glimpse of Natalie tapping away at her keyboard.

A fluke, he thought. He read the next question and carefully chose the answer.

44

WRONG.

The next few minutes seemed like a week. Out of twenty-five questions, he got five wrong. Each one felt like a slap to the head. Who needs to *know* these obscure things? he wanted to shout. His brow was soaked with sweat, his hair a tangled mess. There were five more questions to go. One more wrong, and he would fail.

He cracked his knuckles as the next question appeared on the screen.

Then, like a fingernail scraping on a blackboard, Natalie's voice sang out behind him:

"Finished!"

Never, *never* had Les hated anyone more than his sister at that moment. Hate filled up his brain like water filling a balloon. It clouded his vision and made his jaw clench. He looked at the screen:

26. AT 55 MPH YOU COME UPON A *LARGE* PUDDLE OF WATER. DO YOU:
    A. PUMP YOUR BRAKES?
    B. GENTLY EASE YOUR FOOT OFF THE GAS PEDAL?
    C. ACCELERATE?

His finger hovered over the keyboard, first above A, then above B. He rested his hand off to the side and took a deep breath. Finally, with a burst of energy, he pressed A.

WRONG. YOU HAVE FAILED.

If Les had died right then and there, he probably would have felt a lot better.

Chapter 7

Les's eyes were frozen to the computer screen. His jaw hung open. His hands trembled.

FAILED.

The word cut through him like a knife. To Les, it was more than failing an exam. It was like a cell door slamming in his face. It was a sentence to two more years of adolescent limbo.

The message on the screen glared at him, imprinting itself in his brain like a cattle brand. He couldn't take it . . . he had to wipe it out. . . .

WHACK! Before he could stop himself, he smacked both sides of the computer.

Instantly the screen blipped off. Les looked around. Up and down his row, students stared at their blank screens in shock, their hands shooting into the air.

What have I done now? Les thought. He sank into his seat, mortified.

"Mr. Anderson?" a blue-haired lady called out as she walked through a door that said DEPARTMENT OF MOTOR VEHICLES.

Les shifted from foot to foot, leaning against a counter with a group of other students.

"Yes," he said, in a hushed, defeated voice.

The woman walked up to the counter and smiled at him. "Well, you'll have to thank your sister for this one."

"What do you mean?" he asked.

"At the present moment, the Department of Motor Vehicles' computers are down, so we can't get your test results. However, considering your sister received a perfect score, we're going to pass you, and allow you to take your road test." She shrugged. "How different can you and your twin sister actually be?"

Les's grin was so wide, he felt as if his cheeks would crack.

"Anderson, I want you to take a long, hard look at that cup of coffee."

Les gulped. Mr. Kelly placed a full, steaming cup of coffee on the dashboard of the road-test car. He turned to Les slowly, an ominous sneer on his craggy face. Les couldn't make out Mr. Kelly's eyes behind his aviator sunglasses — but judging from the rest of his face, it was just as well.

"Now, I love my coffee," Mr. Kelly said. "It

47

may be the only thing I truly cherish on this useless mudball we call Earth."

Les nodded nervously.

"What I'm trying to say is that most inspectors use a checklist." He leaned forward in his seat, holding up a clipboard. "I don't believe in them." With a sudden flick of the wrist, he tossed the clipboard out the window. "What I *do* believe in is my cup of coffee. You see, that coffee is hot, filled right to the brim. If it spills on me it'll probably burn me. And no one likes to get burned. So if you burn me, you fail. If you don't, you pass. It's as simple as that."

He sat back into his seat, folding his arms. "Whenever you're ready."

As Les turned the ignition key, he could feel his teeth chatter.

"Okay, Natalie, there's nothing to be nervous about," Natalie's driving instructor said with a smile. "You'll have your license before you know it. Take your time."

Natalie's hands shook. Calm down, she told herself. It's only a driver's license. Let the conformist scions of capitalist America hang their self-worth on this silly piece of plastic.

She put her turn signal on, carefully checked her blind spot, and shifted into first gear.

The instructor grabbed the dashboard as the car jerked forward.

"I'm sorry," she said.

The instructor gave a friendly shrug. "No need to apologize. It happens to everyone."

Natalie drove slowly out of the Department of Motor Vehicles parking lot. To the right was a quiet, hilly street. To the left, horns blared from the main street of Sunny Meadows.

"Now, can you please make a right at the corner?" the instructor asked pleasantly.

"Make a left at the intersection!" Mr. Kelly barked. Les felt as if he were in boot camp. With mounting jealousy, he watched Natalie's car turn slowly *away* from the center of town.

He eased into the street. The coffee swished lazily in the cup, lapping up to the edge — but not over.

Mr. Kelly took a sip and put it back.

On Main Street, cars whizzed from left to right. Les waited for a break in traffic, then turned left into the opposite lane.

WEEEEEEEEOOOOOOOO! Behind him came the ear-splitting wail of an ambulance.

"MOVE TO THE RIGHT!" a voice blasted out through a loudspeaker. *"EMERGENCY! MOVE TO THE RIGHT!"*

Horns blaring around him, Les moved over. The ambulance sped by as Les clutched the steering wheel.

Birds chirped happily as Natalie cruised down Maple Lane. The street was empty except for a few cars parked sparsely at the curb.

"All right," the instructor said. "Stop just up ahead of this car on the right. I'd like you to parallel park."

Natalie stopped by the side of a parked car and turned on her right signal. She checked behind her. The next car was parked so far away she could barely see it.

She pulled in smoothly.

BEEEEEEP!

Les felt as if his throat were coated with sandpaper. The light had flicked from red to green. His eyes darted up to the rearview mirror. The antique car behind him was practically in his trunk. Doesn't that jerk know not to stop so close behind a standard-shift car going uphill? he thought. The minute I take my foot off the brake. . . .

He glanced at the cup on the dashboard. At this angle, the coffee slanted back, barely touching the rim. Droplets of sweat fell off Les's eyebrows. With excruciating care, he released the clutch.

The car moved smoothly forward. Les felt his stomach settle.

Mr. Kelly didn't say a word. He picked up the cup and took another sip, calmly watching the lunch-hour traffic. Then he pointed to the right. "Parallel park — there!"

Les squinted. He couldn't see a parking space — although there *was* a Volkswagen pulling away from a tiny opening.

"There?" Les said, half-jokingly.

Mr. Kelly just glared at him. He obviously wasn't going to repeat himself.

Les signaled and put on his brakes. Behind him, there was a squeal of tires as a whole line of traffic jammed.

To a chorus of horns and curses, Les painstakingly backed into the space. As he pulled in perfectly, Mr. Kelly nodded and said, "Okay, take her back."

Les drove slowly back toward the Department of Motor Vehicles. Relief flooded over him as he finally reached the gates of the parking lot. He headed straight for the nearest empty space.

I have been through the valley of death and survived, he said to himself — without spilling one drop of coffee! It was over. Sixteen years of waiting. Sixteen years of being tied to someone else's timetable. The first thing he would do was drive over to Mercedes's and —

"I got it! I got it!" a voice rang out. Out of nowhere, a girl darted right in front of Les, waving her license to a friend on the other side of the lot.

SCREEEEE! He jammed on the brakes. The car stopped just short of the girl. The coffee cup flew into Mr. Kelly's lap.

Les shot a glance at Mr. Kelly. He opened his mouth, but nothing came out. He couldn't decide whether to plead, scream, or just cry.

Mr. Kelly picked up the cup. He turned it over slowly.

"You're in luck, Anderson," he said. "The cup was empty. See you on the battlefield sometime."

Les had a sudden urge to hug Mr. Kelly. He kept it under control and muttered, "Thank you."

But it was all he could do to keep his knees from buckling as he walked back toward the Department of Motor Vehicles.

Les had wanted to look cool for the camera, as if the whole thing didn't really mean much to him. But as the photographer took aim, he couldn't help but smile like a goon.

"Okay, just wait in line over there," the photographer said. Then he looked at Les's name card. "Anderson . . . say, are you related to a girl named Natalie? She was just here."

"Never heard of her," Les said. He bolted up from the seat and stood in line.

When the attendant handed him his license, he felt frozen to the ground. He fought the urge to scream with happiness, or fall to his knees in gratitude. Instead, he just stared at it, his fingers quivering. Slowly, as if holding a delicate work of art, he began to walk toward the exit.

"Uh, Mr. Anderson?" the attendant called out. "Hold on one second. Someone wants to speak with you."

Les spun around. His eyes widened in horror. The attendant was walking over to the blue-haired lady, pointing to something on a list. Les's heart pounded. One by one, voices echoed in his head:

"Just pass your driver's exam, and then we'll talk," he heard his father say.

"Sure. Call me," came Mercedes's purring voice.

"You're going to be free, Les," Dean insisted. "One of *them* . . . one of *them* . . . one of *them*. . . ."

The old woman approached. Les snapped back to reality. "Well, well. Mr. Anderson, Mr. Anderson," she said rhythmically.

"Yes?" Les answered, his voice little more than a squeak.

The woman's bland face twisted into a vicious smirk. "We were able to retrieve your test results from the computer, Mr. Anderson. And, as I suppose you already know, *you failed!*"

With a sweep of her hand, she presented him with his test results. "God giveth. . . ."

With the other hand, she snatched his license. " . . . and God taketh away. Don't mess with the Department of Motor Vehicles!"

Les felt his blood turn cold as the woman calmly ripped his license to shreds. In shock, he stuffed his test into his back pocket and headed home.

Chapter 8

PICK ME UP! — DEAN
   CONGRATULATIONS, YOU MADE IT!
— CHARLES

Les ripped the phone messages off his bedroom door. He hung his head as he walked inside. On his desk was a gift-wrapped box with a card on top that said *GOOD DRIVING. LOVE, MOM AND DAD.* He tore the box open and pulled out the gift.

A chauffeur's cap.

Les felt tears struggling to pour out. He looked at Mercedes's photo and realized he had never felt worse in his life.

Just then he heard a door slam. "Hello-o-o-o-o! Hello-o-o-o! We're home!"

Great, Les thought. Just when I get to wallow in my own sorrow, I have to face Mom and Dad.

His mind clouded over. He could just see their looks of disappointment and pity. He could feel the sinking sensation of knowing he couldn't borrow the car.

And suddenly Mercedes became a distant, painful memory.

He slogged his way down the hall into a small bedroom. Until this week it had been a storage room, but now it was decked with baby decorations. There, Les's parents were unloading a crib from a cardboard box.

He looked from his mother to his father. There had to be a way. . . .

"Hey, Sport," Mr. Anderson said. "What's the good news?"

Les hung his head. "Mom, Dad, I have something to tell you."

They looked at him expectantly, wide grins on their faces.

And all of a sudden, in a flash of inspiration, he knew just what to do. His frown instantly transformed into a huge grin.

"I'm a freeeeeee man!" he sang out. Pumping his arms triumphantly, he danced around the room. "I'm a freeee man . . . yeaaaaah!"

"Congratulations!" Mrs. Anderson said.

Mr. Anderson laughed. "I filled Mom's car this afternoon, if you feel like taking it for a drive."

Les hadn't planned for that. He stopped dancing. "Uh, no thanks, Dad. I think I'm going to my room to lie down. I'm exhausted."

"Is there something wrong, Les?" his mother said. "Don't you want to take the car for a drive and celebrate a little, get it out of your system?"

"Wrong? Are you kidding? It's just that . . . well, sixteen years of waiting and dreaming is a lot of pressure. It's a powerful moment, and I'm not sure sitting behind the wheel is the place for me to be right now."

"Can we at least *see* your license?" Mrs. Anderson asked.

Les swallowed hard. "Mom, the picture is so ugly, *I'm* even afraid to look at it. It smells."

Mr. Anderson smiled and shook his head. "We're your *parents*, Les. We changed your diapers, remember? I'm quite sure we could handle it."

Les backed out of the room. "Sorry, Dad. It's worse than dirty diapers."

It worked, Les said to himself. He walked down the hallway just as Rudy burst through the front door. He held up his hand and gave Les a high-five.

"Awwrighhhht!" Rudy shouted. "When can we go for a drive?"

"Later, later," Les said. "Let me just make a few phone calls."

He ran into his room and dialed Mercedes's number. Busy.

He hung up the phone — and it immediately rang.

Before he could say hello, he had to take the receiver away from his ear. The sound of recorded cheering blasted into his ear.

"You're the king, Les!" came Dean's voice. "You did it, man! How does it feel?"

"Deano, baby!" Les answered. "Hang on a second, I'm looking for my keys. Wait! Here they are, right beside my AAA card!"

Les's mom smiled. All the way in the basement, she could hear Les singing and whistling in the shower. She held up Les's jeans. She knew he'd be a little angry when he came out of the shower to see them gone, but she also knew he'd want to wear them tonight, and they were filthy. She emptied the pockets, placing the crumpled-up sheet of computer paper on the counter by the washing machine.

Mercedes stretched out on her bed. She surveyed the outfits scattered all around her room. "But why hasn't he called?" she whined into her phone. "He's going to the club tonight, I know it!"

"Mercedes, you could have any guy you'd like," her friend said. "Forget Paolo. He's old enough to be your mother's younger brother."

Les shook his wet hair and closed up his bathrobe. He dialed Mercedes's number, then grimaced as he heard the busy signal again. Quickly he hung up the phone and raced downstairs into the den.

"There you are," Mr. Anderson said, turning from the TV. "Sit down, Chief. I need to talk to you."

With an exuberant smile, Les plopped down on the couch next to Natalie. Mr. Anderson leaned forward solemnly.

"With Mom expecting any day now," he said, "it's extremely important that there is always one car at home. If I'm out, one of you must be here. The same goes for me when the both of you are out. The overriding consideration now is your mother. Am I understood?"

"Yes," said Natalie.

"Absolutely, one hundred percent," Les answered. "Is that all?"

Mr. Anderson handed some photocopied sheets to Les and Natalie. "Now, I've put together a list of the rules of the road that I think we should go over."

"Dad . . . " Les protested.

"This way you'll never be able to say you don't remember hearing them. Take a minute to look them over. They may end up saving your life."

With a reluctant sigh, Les took his sheets and went up to his room. As soon as he closed the door, he pitched them in the trash basket. He rushed over to his tape deck, put on a cassette, and called Mercedes again.

This time the phone rang. Les's pulse quickened.

"Hello . . . ?" The voice was so sexy Les had to sit down.

But before he could open his mouth, the door burst open. Dad stood smiling at him, carrying a bottle of champagne and two glasses.

"Paolo? Is that you?" Mercedes's voice asked.

Les quickly hung up.

"Les, my boy," Mr. Anderson said, "we're drinking a toast to you."

"Dad, that's very thoughtful of you," Les replied, "but you know I shouldn't be drinking and driving."

Mr. Anderson just smiled in answer. He popped open the bottle and poured Les a glass. "Just raise your glass." He held his own glass high in the air. "To saving me twenty-six thousand dollars."

Les raised his glass and took a sip. "I don't get it."

"Twenty-three thousand for the BMW, and three thousand for insurance."

"How did I do that?" Les asked.

"With this." His father casually reached around to his back pocket. He whipped out a sheet of paper.

Les's mouth fell open. Earlier that afternoon, he'd thought nothing could be more painful than seeing the word FAILED lit up on the computer screen.

But seeing it on his test, clutched in his father's hand, was much, much worse.

Chapter 9

"HE *FAILED*?" Natalie's and Rudy's voices echoed into Les's room from the kitchen.

"Sssh," came his mom's voice. Les winced.

Mr. Anderson knelt next to him by the bed. "Les, did it ever occur to you that you could've told your mom and me? We're your parents, not the police."

Les shrugged his shoulders sadly. "I . . . I just figured I could get through the weekend and take the test over Monday." He stared blankly at the wall.

"Come on. It's not the end of the world."

"It feels like it."

Mr. Anderson put his arm around Les. "You'll recover. The great ones always do."

Les nodded, but he hadn't heard the words. All he could think about was Mercedes, and the fact that he had just blown the greatest night of his life.

"I'll get it!" Mrs. Anderson called out. She went to the front door and opened it.

A curly-haired guy smiled up at her. His energetic, dark eyes pierced through his horn-rimmed glasses. "Good evening, Mrs. Anderson. Is Natascha home?"

"She'll be down in a second."

"How are you feeling?"

"Uh, fine, Karl. Thank you."

Karl nodded admiringly. "You have great courage, bringing a child into this oppressive world."

Mrs. Anderson forced a polite smile, but the look on her face said *Get him out of here*. "NATALEEEEEE!" she called out.

Natalie bolted out of her bedroom. "Thanks, Mom," she said, walking out the front door with Karl.

The two of them went over to the driveway, where a beat-up old Citroen awaited them. Natalie hopped in the passenger seat as Karl sat behind the steering wheel and tried to start the car.

The engine sputtered. Natalie rolled her eyes. "Are you sure you don't want to take my mother's Audi? This car's never going to make it to the rally."

Karl flashed a proud grin. "Natascha, don't let this old warrior's heartbeat deceive you. It has more than a lifetime's worth of travel in it."

Mercedes thrashed around her room furiously. She'd already burned her picture of Paolo. All she could do was collapse on her bed with a cry of frustration. Imagine not even *showing up* at the club. . . .

Grinding her teeth, she flipped distractedly through her fashion magazine — until her eyes lit on something scribbled on the front cover. She looked closely. It was a telephone number. . . .

RINNNNNG!

Les lay on his bed, staring at the ceiling. He wondered how long he had been lying there in the dark. It didn't seem to matter much. Nothing really did.

RINNNNNG!

It was only a matter of time now. In a few years, the pot belly would start, then the gray hair, then maybe his nieces and nephews would drive him around. Meanwhile, he had no reason to move. . . .

RINNNNNG!

Les finally became aware of the phone. He plopped a heavy hand on the receiver and slowly picked it up. "Hello."

"Is Les Anderson there?"

The voice sounded familiar. "This is Les."

"Les? This is Mercedes. Mercedes Lane. Remember me?"

Les bolted upright. "Remember you? Ah . . . I'm not sure . . . oh, Mercedes! Of course. How are you?"

"A little lonely, actually."

Les felt his heart stop beating. For a second, he thought he'd died and gone to heaven.

"I thought we had a date this evening. I figured I'd call you, since you hadn't called yet."

"I'm sorry," Les answered, trying to keep his voice from squeaking. "Actually, I was . . . deep-sea fishing all day." He cringed at his own lame excuse.

"You haven't changed your mind, have you?"

"About tonight? Uh . . . no! No!"

"Can you pick me up in twenty minutes?"

Les stiffened with fear.

"Les?"

Les checked the clock. "Hang on," he said. He looked out the window. His mom's Audi 5000 rested peacefully in the driveway, glinting in the moonlight.

He ran into the hall and down to his parents' bedroom. Gently, he pushed the door open. The flickering TV cast its light on the sleeping figures of his mom and dad.

Les, what are you doing? he asked himself. What are you even *thinking*?

He walked back to his room and paused by the phone, his mind racked with doubts.

Finally he picked up the receiver.

"Mercedes? I'll be there in half an hour."

"Great. And Les? Can you bring some liquor?" Her voice became a sultry purr. "Vodka drives me *crazy*!"

Chapter 10

The crickets' chirping mixed with the sound
of an old rerun as Les gently tiptoed to his
father's night table. The keys sat in plain
sight on top. They seemed to dance in the
light of the TV. Les inched his fingers toward
them.

Suddenly, like a whale rolling up out of the
dark sea, Mr. Anderson's silhouette moved in
the bed. Les recoiled.

Thwock! Les watched in horror as his
father's hand landed on top of the keys.
Swallowing a gasp, Les looked at his dad.

Mr. Anderson's eyes were closed tight. He
hadn't awakened for a second.

Les backed slowly out of the room. He ran
downstairs to the kitchen and rummaged
through a desk drawer that always contained
the spare keys.

Not this time. He searched through the
other drawers, his mind racing. Where else
could a set of car keys be?

Car keys — of course! Les flew out the front door and ran to the garage. The turquoise Cadillac gleamed even in the darkness. He peeked in the front window.

There, dangling from the steering column, was the set of keys.

"Anderson, you're a genius," Les said softly.

He ran back inside, to his parents' liquor cabinet. There he filled an empty flask with vodka and poured some ice into a cooler.

He sped back out to the garage and quietly opened its door. Once in, he lay the flask and cooler by the trunk, then pulled open the car's front door.

WEEEEEEEEEEEEEEOOOOOOOOO!

He plunged into the car and flicked off the alarm. Curling up in the front seat, he waited for his parents, like a death row prisoner waiting for his turn in the chair.

After what seemed like an hour, no one responded. Les sat up and looked around. The coast was clear. He turned the ignition part way, unlocking the steering wheel. Then he shifted the car into neutral and stepped outside.

With all his weight, he leaned against the hood of the car and pushed.

Slowly it began rolling down the incline of the driveway. Les ran alongside and reached for the door handle. He fumbled with it as the car picked up speed, rolling faster . . . faster. . . .

Les grabbed frantically for the door, but the car was out of control. It swerved to the right, backing across the Andersons' front lawn.

Les held his breath as the Caddy plowed through the perfectly trimmed front hedges, leaving a seven-foot gap and a double scar of tire tracks on the lawn. Then, with a thud, it bounced to a stop against the curb.

There wasn't even time to think. Moving as fast as he could, Les propped up the hedges and stomped on the tire tracks. Then he sprinted back to the garage, unscrewed all the lightbulbs, and hit the automatic door control.

As the garage door slowly shut behind him, Les ran to the Caddy, hopped in, and drove away.

Minutes later, Karl's Citroën came sputtering up to the Anderson's driveway. Natalie rubbed her forehead in frustration. "Karl, if you're not convinced this car's about to die, maybe we should wait until it catches fire and cremates itself."

"Need you be so cruel, Natascha?" Karl said.

Natalie rolled her eyes. "Let me just get the keys to my mother's Audi."

As Karl sulked in the car, Natalie stepped out and went inside the house. She sneaked into her parents' room and spotted the keys under her father's hand.

Without a moment's hesitation, she lifted his hand and pulled the key to the Audi off the ring, being careful to leave the Caddy keys.

Mr. Anderson's eyes popped open. Natalie returned his startled look with a calm gaze. She held out the key.

He smiled peacefully and fell back to sleep, and Natalie slipped back into the hallway.

She was already down the stairs when the bedroom light suddenly flicked on. And she was climbing in the car with Karl when her mother sat up abruptly in bed with a shooting pain in her abdomen.

"I'm not so sure this is a good idea," Karl said.

"I'm not, either," Natalie answered, turning on the ignition. "But we have to get there, right?"

"Yes, but your mother — "

"It's okay. My grandfather's car is in the garage." With that, Natalie put the Audi in gear and backed into the street.

In the bedroom, Mrs. Anderson sat up and breathed deeply. She looked over at her husband, who was fast asleep. When the pain subsided, she let out a sigh of relief and shut the light.

I want a justice of the peace — now! Les thought when Mercedes came to her front door. But all he could say was a feeble, "You look great."

"Thanks. You look cute," Mercedes answered, with a killer smile.

Les ran out to the Caddy and held open the door for her. Then he jumped in, popped a tape in the deck, and started the car. Mercedes threw her head back, swaying to the music, as Les backed into the street.

"So where do you feel like going?" he asked.

"I know the perfect place," Mercedes said. "You'll love it." She cranked up the tape deck to an ear-splitting level, just as a car pulled up beside them.

Les looked over — right into the faces of two cops. Terror shot through him as he lowered the volume.

He felt his head spinning. He could hear the judge intoning in court: "For driving without a license in a stolen car with a flask of vodka under the seat — three concurrent sentences of forty years each!"

He smiled and shrugged at the cops. They looked at Les, looked at Mercedes, smiled, and drove off.

That had been too close for comfort. With a shudder, Les began to think this wasn't such a great idea, after all.

Minutes later, Les edged the car down the streets of a seedy-looking neighborhood. Ahead of them, the name EL REY'S glowed above a small building. Les watched as a valet hopped into a car in front of the club.

The tires squealed as the car lurched toward the parking lot, leaving a cloud of blue smoke.

Another valet headed toward the Caddy. Les hit the automatic door lock. "I'll park it myself," he said.

Les crept past the club and turned into an alley. He eyed the cars parked on either side — smashed windows, broken glass. All of a sudden he wished he were in an armored tank.

Mercedes swigged at the flask, then sat up excitedly. "There's one!" she said.

Les looked over. A huge, gaping space was bathed in the light of a bright street lamp. It couldn't have been more perfect.

He drove up and glided right in. But his heart sank as he looked up at a sign on the lamppost.

NO STOPPING. TOW ZONE.

"I can't park here," he said, just as Mercedes reached for the door handle. She gave him a baffled look, and he pointed to the sign.

"It's Saturday night!" Mercedes said. "Les, nobody tows cars on a weekend. Look at all the cars behind us. You think they're worried?"

Les looked back timidly. Somehow the other cars didn't comfort him at all.

Mercedes laughed. "Relax. You're acting like it's the first time you've ever driven."

That did it. No *way* was Les going to let his cover be blown. Besides, Mercedes sounded as if she knew what she was talking about — parking rules were probably things only experienced drivers knew about. With a confident, rakish smile, he shut off the ignition and got out of the car.

In front of the club stood a swarm of people, anxiously eyeing the front door. They huddled around as a doorman came out and peered at their faces, bored. Then he leaned up against the doorjamb and stared into the distance, without letting anyone in.

Mercedes sashayed toward the crowd, her hair rippling in the breeze. Les followed on her heels.

The doorman's face broke into a grin when he saw her. "Yo, babe, go ahead," he said, waving her in.

"Thanks, Bruno," she replied.

Amazing! Les thought. The world falls to its knees for her — and she's *my* date!

He threw his shoulders back and walked past the doorman. "Yo, Bruno," he said.

But a sudden, vicelike grip on his arm stopped him in his tracks. "Where you goin'?" Bruno said.

Les whipped around. "Hey, come on, I'm with her."

Bruno nodded, tightening his grip. "Riiiiight," he said. "You wouldn't be with her if she were your Siamese twin. Now, run along before someone steals your tricycle, Mikey."

Les looked up at Bruno's hard-set jaw.

He toyed with the idea of fighting back, but realized he valued his teeth too much. All he could do was smile wanly and watch Mercedes's slinky figure disappear into the vortex of people inside.

Chapter 11

I *knew* he'd be here, Mercedes said to herself. She turned her head so Paolo wouldn't see her. Her eyes lit on a stiff drink, resting on a napkin in front of a guy at the bar. With a quick sweep of her arm, she grabbed the drink and downed it.

She felt her face flush. Steadying herself, she approached Paolo.

Paolo raised an eyebrow when he saw her. "Mercedes, what a lovely surprise," he said with an oily smile. "Where is your high-school heartthrob?"

Mercedes spun around. Les was nowhere to be seen. She wasn't expecting that. She felt her courage start to slip away.

When she turned back, a sexy redhead was slithering up to Paolo. With a devilish smile, the girl draped her arms around his shoulders and nibbled on his ear.

Mercedes's stomach started to turn.

Paolo took a bottle of champagne from a table and poured a glass. "Please, Mercedes. Sit down and join us for something to drink."

"No, thanks," Mercedes answered through clenched teeth. "But here's something to go with it."

The sound of her hand smacking Paolo's face carried all the way outside, where Les was staring in through a window. He grinned with satisfaction.

Mercedes grabbed Paolo's magnum of champagne, spun on her heel, and stormed out.

Les ran around to the front of El Rey's, just as Mercedes emerged. Swigging the champagne, she stomped right by him toward the car.

Les followed behind her. "Merce —" he began to call out.

But his mouth locked in the middle of the word. The Caddy was beginning to pull away from his parking space — hooked up to a tow truck!

Les sprinted into the street. On both sides of him, cars screeched to a stop and swerved away. The sound of angry horns filled the night air as Les stood in front of the tow truck, arms outstretched.

A beefy, craggy-faced driver stuck his head out the window. He narrowed his eyes at Les and said, "Get out of the way, boy."

Les jumped onto the truck's hood. "You can't do this to my car!"

The truck began rolling forward. Les clutched onto the hood. "Boy," the driver grumbled, "I've driven with deers, antelopes, even bears strapped to my bumper. A sixty-five-pound sack of fluff like you ain't gonna make a bit of a difference."

"Please!" Les shouted. "I'll do anything. I can pay you. I'll give you everything I have!"

The truck jerked to a stop. Les flew over the hood and tumbled onto the street.

He sprang to his feet to see the driver slamming the door behind him. "Okay, pay up," he said, his palms out.

Les emptied his pockets and laid the bills in the driver's hand. "Here — twenty . . . forty . . . sixty . eighty. Now be gentle. Please!"

The driver walked around to the back of the truck. "For eighty dollars?"

He hit a switch, and the Cadillac crashed down onto the ground. Les grimaced.

With a gravelly laugh, the driver jumped in his truck and pulled away.

Les walked toward the Caddy, shaking. Mercedes belted down a huge gulp of champagne and approached him, holding out the bottle. "Here," she said, "this might help."

"No, thanks," Les answered. He thought back to his father's champagne toast. "I already had some tonight."

"I'm really sorry about this. I feel like it was all my fault."

"Nah, I should've given the car to the valet." He looked away from her and added quietly, "It's too bad about your friend."

Mercedes gave a dismissive wave of her hand. "He was a jerk, anyway. I don't know why I even hung around with him." She looked at the Caddy, then at Les. Her face glowed. "Why don't we get out of here?"

"And go where? With the amount of money I have left in my pocket, we have two choices. Sit at a parking meter for twenty minutes, or go buy ourselves a paper."

Mercedes laughed, her eyes like blue flames. "I know a quiet spot, with plenty of free parking."

"Hic!" With each hiccup, Mercedes burst into giggles and took another swig of champagne.

The Caddy bounced up and down as it scaled a narrow, uphill dirt road. Les gritted his teeth and yanked the steering wheel right and left, trying in vain to avoid low-hanging branches. He regretted ever having taken Mercedes's suggestion.

"Hic! Are we there yet?" Mercedes said in a voice much louder than it needed to be.

Soon the trees began to thin out. Les slowed the car down as it reached the top of the mountain.

Suddenly he found himself driving into a clearing. He stopped the car and gaped at the view out the windshield. Below them the city stretched out, like a million glowing diamonds.

Les got out and checked the car's paint. It didn't seem scratched at all. Then the passenger door slammed shut and Mercedes staggered out, clutching the champagne bottle. Les noticed it was three-quarters empty.

They both leaned against the car and stared upward. The stars above seemed to mirror the lights of the city below. Like a giant white cloud, the Milky Way slashed across the sky.

"This is unbelievable up here," Les said. "How did you find this place?"

Mercedes closed her eyes. A tipsy, dreamy smile crept across her face. "Someone I know used to take me here."

Les turned away, crushed. He should have known. . . .

"Not a boyfriend," she said, with a knowing glance. "My father used to bring me here to show me how pretty the world could be if you step away and see it from a distance." She sighed. "I haven't been here in a long time." She stumbled toward the front of the car and began to lean against it.

"Wait!" Les shouted. He dove between her and the car. "I have a blanket. It'll be more comfortable." He raced around to the trunk, got the blanket, and spread it out on the hood.

Mercedes draped her body over the blanket and drank down some more champagne.

"Mmm," she said. "All we're missing is some soft, romantic music."

With a grin, Les sprang into action. He pulled a cassette tape out of his pocket and checked the label he'd written on it: MERCEDES — SLOW. Pulling open the car door, he sat inside and snapped the tape into the deck.

A plaintive ballad throbbed through the speakers. Les adjusted the volume. He watched Mercedes throw her head back blissfully, swaying to the music. His blood began to race. He slipped out of the car. Then. . . .

"BEEEE-WOOOP-BRAAAAP — "

Les fell back in and ejected the cartridge. Chewed-up brown cassette tape spilled all over the front seat. Frantically he turned on the radio.

"SSSS . . . CCHHH . . . Sixty degrees tonight . . . SSS. . . ."

Useless.

Les shut it off and pulled open the glove compartment. A row of cassettes stared back at him. I'm in luck, he thought. Then he read the labels: COMO, BENNETT, TORME, SINATRA, HUMPERDINCK.

I'm *not* in luck, he realized. This is the geriatric hit parade.

In desperation, he put on a Sinatra tape. As he stepped out of the car, a lush orchestral arrangement filled the night air:

"*Strangers in the night, exchanging glances. . . .*"

The music may have been prehistoric, but

somehow it was just right for the occasion. He leaned on the hood next to Mercedes. She drank the last few drops of champagne, then closed her eyes.

Suddenly Les's hands felt like lead weights. He had no idea what to do with them. He took a tentative step closer to her.

Mercedes gazed at him with heavy, sensual eyes. "Do you want to dance?"

Before Les could stop her, she climbed on top of the hood. Her stiletto heels clacked against the metal.

Les blanched. This was just what he needed. By the time he drove home, the hood was going to look like the dark side of the moon! But he couldn't think of that now. He carefully climbed up next to Mercedes. She undulated from side to side. Les tried to undulate with her. She moved closer . . . closer. . . . Les found himself staring into her collar bone. He stood on his toes.

"Maybe I should take my shoes off," Mercedes suggested gently. She knelt down. When she stood back up, she was eye-to-eye with Les.

The music soared. So did Les's spirits. He felt his body being drawn to hers.

He wrapped his arms around her. She clutched and unclutched the back of his shirt, responding to his every move. Slowly they sank down on the hood, lost in each other's embrace.

"It turned out so right," Sinatra's voice sang, *"for strangers in the...."*

Thump.

The noise sounded like a bass drum, but it wasn't. A bass drum wouldn't have made their bodies jolt downward.

Les yanked himself away. "Get up," he ordered. "Get off the hood!"

"What's the matter?" Mercedes asked, sliding off.

"The hood is caving in. Quick, get off!" He took off the blanket. A wide, gaping dent stared up at him. "Oh, no. I'll be making repair payments from Siberia."

He jumped into the car. Maybe Dean could fix it. Mercedes fell in beside him. He tried to start up the engine, but Mercedes grabbed his hand. She pulled herself toward him, kissing him. Les tried to struggle — but only briefly.

He smiled. It couldn't get much better than this — or could it?

Suddenly he got his answer. Mercedes passed out.

This isn't happening to me, Les said to himself.

And as if in answer, Sinatra's voice began a new song: *"That's life ... that's what the people say...."*

Chapter 12

Pam-pam-pam-pam. Les and Charles watched as Dean pounded out the dent with a mallet. Pulling himself out from under the Caddy's hood, Dean looked up at the work he'd done. "You definitely have guts for snatching this car, Les," he said. "I'm impressed."

"Let's see the license," Charles blurted out, grabbing his camera. "I want to take a picture."

"It's ugly," Les protested.

"Of course it is," Dean said. "Big deal."

"Oh, okay." Les took out his wallet, opened it, and whipped his student I.D. right in front of Charles's camera as the flash went off. There was no way the camera would pick anything up.

Dean put his mallet down and gently dropped the hood. "Take a look."

Les smiled. It was as good as new. "Excellent work, Dean. You saved me."

"So I guess we can go to Archie's tonight?" Dean said.

"Dean, I promised next weekend. Not tonight. There's still a couple of hours before Mercedes has to be home."

Dean looked down at Mercedes, fast asleep in the passenger seat. "Les, this Mercedes has a dead battery," he said. "Look, Archie's is in the middle of nowhere. You can't get there without a license. No buses, no trains, no planes. Only the slickest driving machines you've ever seen."

"How do you know it's any good?" Charles asked. "You've never been there."

"Charles," Dean retorted. "Do I tell you what kind of dictionaries to buy?"

"I don't know, Dean," Les said. "I'm a little tired. I don't feel like driving on the highway."

"What? You got your license twelve hours ago and you're already tired of driving? My *mother* makes ridiculous statements like that."

"Forget it, Dean. I just can't."

Dean grabbed his mallet. Like an executioner with an ax, he lifted it high into the air over the Caddy's hood. "Can't?"

Dean nestled in the backseat next to the sleeping Mercedes as Les backed out of the driveway. Pulling three cigars out of his pocket, he said, "Charles, push in the lighter. I have a surprise for everyone."

"No way, Dean," Les said.

"Les, this is a car, not an oxygen tent."

"Forget it. If there's even the slightest evidence that I took this car, my dad will slaughter first and ask questions later."

Dean scowled and fell silent as Les drove through the streets.

Crawled would have been a better description. Cars passed them left and right. Dean groaned as a jogger sped by them. "A bath is more exciting than this," he muttered.

Ignoring him, Les carefully turned onto Main Street and stopped at a red light. By now, Dean was ready to burst.

Just then, to the right of them, a raucous car horn blared a funeral march. They all spun around to see a primer gray GTO rumble to a stop. In the window were three familiar, leering faces — the three goons who had taunted Dean and Les Thursday before the party.

The driver revved his engine, challenging Les to a drag race. Dean smirked at him. Les revved *his* engine.

The light flicked to green, and the GTO screeched away, leaving a cloud of burned rubber.

Les edged forward cautiously, letting the other car disappear into the distance.

"What?" Dean screamed. "Les, are you sixteen, or are you sixty? You could have given that gear-head a run for his money!"

"Dean," Les said, "this is my grandfather's car."

Dean flopped back into his seat. "It feels like your grandfather's driving it."

Les could practically see the steam rising from the backseat as he continued to trundle along.

"Honey . . . honey?"

Mr. Anderson could have slept through the gentle plea, but not the shoving. He felt as if he'd been awakened by a sledgehammer. "Huh?" was all he could muster for an answer.

"Is it hot in here or is it just me?" his wife asked.

"It's you," Mr. Anderson grunted.

"Oh, it feels like a sauna!"

Out of his half-open eyes, Mr. Anderson could see perspiration dripping down his wife's forehead. Groggily, he pushed himself up from the bed. "Okay, I'll go down to the garage and turn on the air-conditioning."

He stumbled downstairs and into the backyard. Like a zombie, he walked to the garage door and lifted it open.

With a yawn, he peered inside. It was pitch-black. He reached in and flicked on the light switch. Nothing happened.

Gotta fix that wiring, he said to himself. He shut the door behind him and shuffled back toward the house. In the kitchen he pulled a flashlight out of a drawer, then headed back out to the garage.

Guiding himself with the flashlight, he stopped right in front of the door and knelt down to open it.

Just as his hand gripped the handle, a crackling voice made him jump back.

"Robert? Robert?"

He looked at the molding on the door, where the intercom rested. "Yes, dear."

"I changed my mind. I'm not hot any longer. I'm hungry. Can you make me a herring-and-mayonnaise sandwich?"

Mr. Anderson started to feel queasy.

" . . . with extra bacon bits?"

Click. The light from the camera's flashbulb filled the Caddy. Charles and Les spun around. Dean was positioning himself to take another picture of Mercedes.

"You jerk!" Les yelled. "Put that away! Now!"

Dean laughed and sat back. "Look at us. Three wild animals bombing down the highway in a Cadillac with the cruise control set on fifty-five."

"Well, excuse me, that's the speed limit. I don't need a ticket my first night out."

"A ticket?" Dean bellowed. "Look at your windshield. We're moving so slowly the flies have time to get out of the way."

"Dean, you need a doctor," Charles said.

Click. Dean took another picture.

That was the last straw. Les reached back with his arm. "Give me the camera, Dean!"

Dean pulled away and snapped another photo. Les lunged behind him and grabbed the camera, taking his eyes off the road. Dean jerked his arms away, pulling Les out of his seat. The Caddy began to swerve. Frantically Charles tried to separate them.

Suddenly the flash went off — right in Les's eyes.

"Aaargh!" Les cried out.

Their bodies pitched from side to side as the car skidded all over the road. Dean let out a whoop of laughter.

When Les opened his eyes, he might as well have been on Jupiter. All he could see was a purple landscape.

He gripped the steering wheel and prayed. When his vision cleared, the first thing he made out was a green sign whizzing by them. He squinted and read the words:

EXIT

REDUCE SPEED TO TWENTY

Les panicked. The car was bombing toward a busy intersection. In the middle of it, an enormous puddle shone with the reflection of the streetlights.

Before Les could react, three computer-printed choices popped into his head — choices that were just as frightening now as they were on his driver's ed test:

A. PUMP YOUR BRAKES?

B. GENTLY EASE YOUR FOOT OFF
   THE GAS PEDAL?

C. ACCELERATE?

The one he had chosen was wrong — but which was it?

His reflexes took over. He jammed on the brakes.

The Caddy spun wildly. Dean and Charles clutched onto the sides of the car. The surroundings became a blur. Cars screeched onto the sidewalk to avoid them. The Caddy slid through the intersection — backward. Water gushed up all around them, coating the windshield. Les whipped the car around and reached for the wipers.

With a swift flick, the wiper blades cleared the view — a view of a speeding truck's headlights.

HONNNNNNNK!

Les screamed. He yanked the steering wheel to the left.

The car cut across the oncoming traffic and onto the shoulder. Dean and Charles shielded their eyes as they barreled toward a plywood fence.

SPLLAAAAACCCCK! Shards of wood flew around them as the Caddy plowed right through.

Suddenly Les's mouth opened in a silent scream. Below them, the ground slipped away — and the car hurtled through the air like a DC-10 without landing gear!

Chapter 13

Dean howled with joy. Charles screamed with horror. Les closed his eyes and hoped there really was such a thing as reincarnation.

The Caddy plummeted to the ground. With a sickening, metallic *crrrunch*, it landed on a soft, grassy hill.

Les's eyes opened in disbelief. Blades of tall grass whisked by them. The car was still plunging ahead, and they were all alive!

So far.

With a sudden *whoosh*, the grass gave way. Now Les could see ahead of him — right into the windows of a restaurant.

Les stomped on the brakes. The restaurant loomed larger as they skidded across the parking lot.

And they all lurched forward and back as the car slid perfectly into a space next to a station wagon.

For a long moment, Les sat motionless.

Only his eyes moved, doing a quick check. His hands were still there . . . so was the windshield . . . that meant his head was intact. . . .

He looked slowly to his right. Charles was there, in one piece, his face the color of chalk. He checked the backseat.

Dean's grinning face peered up at Les. Mercedes had fallen on top of him, still unconscious. Her lips were slightly parted, inches away from his. He puckered his lips and maneuvered his face closer to hers . . . and closer.

Just then Mercedes stirred. In a groggy, thick voice, she said, "I have to throw up."

Dean recoiled in horror.

Les spun around. "Open the door!" he yelled. "Get her out!"

"I can't!" Dean screamed. "I'm trapped! Help me!"

Les jumped out of the car, pulled open the back door, and tore Mercedes away from Dean. "Not in the car, please," he said.

Mercedes slid to the ground in an unconscious stupor. Charles staggered out of the car as if all his bones were broken.

But Dean was smiling when he bounced out the back door. He gave Les an admiring glance. "I apologize for everything, Bro. That ride made up for a whole life of boredom." Stretching, he walked out to the sidewalk.

But Les didn't hear a word. His eyes full

of dread, he surveyed the grime-encrusted car.

"I think the muck saved the paint," Charles said.

"We need a car wash and then we're going home," Les answered.

Dean ran up to him, his eyes on fire. "Les, we're almost at Archie's. We can't turn back now. Besides. . . ." He looked down at Mercedes, who let out a moan. " . . . I don't think you want her in your car. She's about to blow."

"He's right," Charles said, glancing at the restaurant. "It wouldn't hurt to get her a soda."

Dean pointed to the restaurant's wall. Les and Charles followed his finger to see a coiled water hose. "Look, Les," Dean said. "We can hose the car down while Charles takes Mercedes in there for something to drink."

To Les, it was the smartest thing Dean had said all night. "Charles?" he said.

Charles blushed. He looked at Mercedes as if she were an exotic species of animal he'd never seen before. With a sigh of resignation, he said, "Sure."

He gathered up Mercedes and carried her toward the side entrance, his face turning redder as she muttered into his ear.

As soon as they disappeared into the restaurant, Dean grabbed Les by the arm. "I want you to see something." He walked him to the sidewalk.

Across the street, high on a platform under a garish neon sign that said SICK SAM'S 24-HOUR RENT-A-CAR, was a Cadillac — a turquoise '72 Sedan De Ville, absolutely identical to the car Les was driving.

"Now," Dean said, "look up there and tell me what's on your mind."

"Death," Les said flatly.

Dean gave him a sly, piercing look. "I just want you to *think* about it, Les."

"Think about what?" Les said. But he didn't want to hear the answer. He turned back toward the parking lot and headed straight for the hose.

As Dean patiently looked on, Les washed the car. To his amazement, under all the dirt it had practically no scratches.

"You were lucky," Dean said. He ran his finger along the car. "Real lucky. Wouldn't it be great if we didn't have to worry about this car?" He gestured toward the rent-a-car place.

Les stared at him. "You're not insane enough to suggest — "

"Les, it's perfect! No one would know the difference. The car is a clone! Exactly the same year, color, wheels, everything!"

Les was outraged. He could feel the veins in his neck pop out. "Are you out of your mind?" he yelled. "I will *not* switch cars! You're a nut!"

"You'll never get an opportunity like this again, as long as you live. We'll cruise up to

Archie's without worrying about scratching the paint, dirtying the interior, or smashing the car. If you ask me, it's a sign from the Mr. Goodwrench in the sky." He began walking toward the street.

Les followed him. "I don't believe in Mr. Goodwrench," he said.

"There's still time to convert."

Now the other Caddy was in plain sight. Les had to admit, it was tempting. . . .

"You worked real hard for that license you have in your wallet," Dean said, walking reverently toward the car lot. "You've had sixteen years of humiliation, begging for lifts from people who couldn't care less about your image. You had to stand and watch as all the pretty girls in our grade drove away smiling in some older jerk's car — and you had to grin and bear it when the girl of your dreams asked you what kind of car you drove. But that's all over now."

He stopped just below the Cadillac ramp. Les gazed up at the gleaming turquoise car in awe. "That thing in your wallet is not just an ordinary piece of paper, Les," Dean went on. "It's not even just an automobile license. It's a license to live. Did you hear me, Les? A license to live, to be free — to go wherever you want, whenever you want, with whoever you choose." He looked Les straight in the eye. "It is the single most liberating document you'll come across in your whole life. I would die to have one."

Les felt himself nod. It was hard not to agree.

"Les," Dean pressed, "to live in fear is not to live at all."

"What about getting the car back?"

"A breeze. If the attendant's awake, we use Charles as a decoy. He looks old enough."

Les looked past Dean to the building. Through the window, he saw an old man fast asleep in a chair. A lone strand of hair was slicked across his otherwise bald head, and on his lapel was the name Sick Sam. The scratchy sound of easy-listening music wafted out of his radio.

"How are we going to get past him?" Les said.

Dean smiled confidently. He walked quietly toward the office door. Les followed close behind, keeping a wary eye on Sick Sam. Behind Sam, keys hung on a board. One of them was marked '72 CADDY. Opposite the board, to Sam's left, was a hole in the wall. Les figured Sam used that to talk to people outside.

Dean tried the door. It was locked. He turned to Les and shrugged helplessly.

Les put up his index finger, signaling Dean to wait. He ran across the street to his grandfather's Caddy, opened the trunk, and reached into the golf bag.

He took out a long, three-pronged ball fetcher. He had seen his grandfather use it to pull balls out of the tiny holes on a golf course. It would be perfect for this. He ran back to the building, to the other side of the hole.

Dean's face was intense with excitement as Les pushed the instrument through the hole. He extended his arm as far as he could. The fetcher closed around the keys, barely grasping them. Slowly, he lifted the keys off the hook. . . .

Chinkle! Les and Dean ducked below the hole as the keys fell off the fetcher.

Les carefully peeked back through. The keys had landed squarely on Sick Sam's shoulders, without waking him up.

Taking a deep breath, Les maneuvered the fetcher toward Sick Sam.

It made a metallic noise as it closed firmly around the key ring. The keys tinkled as they rose off Sick Sam's shoulder. Les pulled the keys toward them, trying to keep his hand as steady as possible. When he finally pulled them outside, he beamed at Dean.

"Okay, let's go!" he said, starting back toward the restaurant.

Dean turned to follow him, then stopped. He turned back to the hole. Sticking his hand through, he turned up the volume on Sick Sam's radio.

Les ran up the ramp and into the car. He shut the door behind him, shifted into neutral, and let the car roll backward down the ramp. When he was on level ground, Dean pushed him out of the lot.

Then Les darted back across the street and drove his grandfather's car onto the ramp. He and Dean took the golf clubs, cooler, and blanket, and put them in the other car. Using the ball fetcher again, he replaced his own keys on Sick Sam's hook.

Les felt like he'd pulled off the crime of the century. It looked as though absolutely nothing had happened. Both he and Dean grinned from ear to ear as they walked toward the restaurant to fetch Charles and Mercedes.

In the rental office, Sick Sam's eyes flickered open. He wasn't sure, but he thought he'd heard something outside. He walked over to the window and peered out into the lot. No one was around. The Cadillac was still sitting on the ramp.

From this angle, Sick Sam hadn't seen the one thing that made the car different — the license plate with the word GRANDPA.

Yawning, he walked back to his desk and plopped down into his chair. Before he drifted into sleep, he reached instinctively into his half-open top drawer.

The revolver was still there. Just in case.

Chapter 14

Mercedes's limp body was growing heavy in Les's arms. He watched impatiently as Dean opened the Cadillac's trunk.

Les looked into its vast blackness and shook his head. "I don't know if this is a good idea," he said.

"What are you talking about?" Dean replied, taking a bite of a steaming slice of pizza. "In a half hour there's gonna be babes all over us. She'll kill it for us." He and Charles removed the golf clubs and cooler and threw them in the backseat.

Reluctantly, Les placed Mercedes in the trunk. Her eyes fluttered, then shut again. And as Les tenderly covered her with the blanket, she cuddled up with a blissful, unknowing smile.

"In all your life," Dean said, "did you ever imagine you'd see a Mercedes fit in the trunk of a Cadillac?"

"I feel bad," Les answered, his hand resting on the lid of the trunk. "I can't lock her in there."

"All right, already," Dean snapped. "Let's tie the lid so it stays open, if you insist!"

"I still feel bad," Les said.

Dean gave him a disbelieving glance. "For her? That trunk is bigger than my bedroom."

Gently Les pushed down the lid, using some rope to keep it open a crack.

"WooooOOOOO-HAAAAA!" Dean wailed. His voice cut through the rock music that boomed from the car radio.

Les floored the accelerator. The cups of soda on the dashboard shook. He looked in the rearview mirror and grinned at Dean's image — funky sunglasses, a corny golf visor, and a huge, gooey slice of pizza hanging from his mouth.

"Whoops!" Dean said. "I just dropped some pizza on the seat."

"Leave it, Deano," Les answered casually. "I'll get it later."

Charles turned to him in shock. "What's going on? An hour ago you were afraid one of us would *breathe* in here, and now you don't even flinch when Dean drops tomato sauce on the seats. Don't you care about what happens to your own grandfather's car?"

Poor, unsuspecting kid, Les thought. "Sure I care," he said. "But there's something special about tonight, Charles. About Mercedes, about the car surviving the spinout without even a scratch — about *us*, being in a car alone without any parents. Charles, we've been waiting for this night for *sixteen* years. If I have to worry about smoke and tomato sauce now, when I'm twenty-five I'll be living in a room with rubber walls."

Dean leaned over and cranked up the volume on the radio. "RELAX, CHARLES!" he howled. "THERE'S NOTHING TO WORRY ABOUT!"

In another, much quieter part of town, Mrs. Anderson stared at her TV set, licking the remnants of a herring-mayo-bacon bits sandwich off her fingers. A ragged chanting of voices came from a news broadcast:

"WE ARE ONE WITH THE INFINITE SUN. . . ."

Standing in front of a group of people holding placards, a newswoman raised a microphone to her lips and said, "I'm standing here outside the gates of Allied Technologies, where a group of peaceful protesters has gathered to demonstrate against the late-night transportation of military hardware through our streets. . . ."

Natalie looked around nervously as police cars began pulling up alongside the camera crews. "Karl, I don't have a good feeling about this. Can we go home?"

Karl stopped chanting and turned to her.

"Go home? Natascha, we can't be patsies to the military-industrial complex. The survival of the planet is in our hands."

Natalie had come to this rally full of conviction. But looking at those policemen, coming out of their cars with billy clubs strapped to their belts, she wasn't so sure.

"Are you sure this is the way?" Les asked over his shoulder. A long, deserted highway stretched in front of them — as it had for miles.

Dean looked down at a crumpled sheet of paper. "Relax, my brother's been here millions of times. He wouldn't steer us — " He cut himself off as his eyes darted toward the horizon. "That must be it! Look!"

An eerie neon glow loomed high above a distant grove of trees. Les gunned the car, and he bombed down the next exit ramp.

Just up the road to the right, the sign was clear: ARCHIE'S ATOMIC BROILER. Dean whooped with joy as loud rock music pierced the air, drowning out even their own stereo.

As Les drove closer, he stared with wonder. Archie's was a glittering neon-and-chrome masterpiece — a slice of the fifties gone high tech. Dozens of BMWs, Maseratis, and Porsches idled at curbside in front. He had to squint at the light reflected off their polish. Each car had a tray full of food attached to a front-door window. Kids flocked around each tray, laughing, dancing, and eating.

Girls on roller skates glided in and out between the cars, their hair flowing in the breeze. Bumping and grinding to the music, some of them were practically bursting out of their skimpy outfits.

On one side of Archie's there was a long line of people waiting to order food. On the other side, three incredible-looking girls stared at the Caddy with toothpaste-ad smiles.

Les felt like dancing with joy. He pulled up to the only empty spot in the place.

Dean's head popped between him and Charles. "Order for me," he said. "I'll get dessert."

As Les and Charles went to get food, Dean swaggered off toward the girls.

Carrying two trays that spilled over with burgers, fries, and Pepsis, Les and Charles rushed to the car and attached them to its sides. They hopped in the front seat just as Dean returned.

"It's all set," Dean said, jumping in the backseat with a huge grin. "They'll be here in a couple of minutes. One for each of us."

Les passed out the fries and Pepsis. "My dreams never get this good," he said.

"My fantasies never get this good," Dean answered. "And this is only the beginning."

"I'll never doubt you again, Dean," Charles said, his eyes lit up with excitement. He flung his hand out the window for a burger. His hand knocked against a salt shaker and sent it flying onto the ground. Dazed and hungry, Charles pushed open his door.

Chunk! The door rammed against the car next to them. Les looked across at it — and his heart jumped.

It was an all-too-familiar gray car. A *primer gray* GTO.

Slowly, ominously, the GTO's door opened. Like a crocodile emerging from a swamp, the driver got out and glowered at Charles. His friends joined him, swigging from bottles of whiskey. Together they crowded around the tiny dent in their car as if they were examining a mortal wound.

"It's those maniacs from the party," Les said.

"Quick! Roll up the windows!" Charles screamed, closing his window on Dean's hand just as he reached out for a burger.

"Charles, you idiot!" Dean yelled. He pulled his hand back in as Charles rolled down the window a fraction of an inch, then shut it tight.

The three of them stared helplessly out the windows at the faces of three grizzled, homicidal maniacs. The driver leaned back toward his car and reached in through an open window.

When he pulled his hand out, it was clutching an enormous tire iron. His face broke into an evil smile. Then, with a wave of his index finger, he signaled for the three guys to get out of the car.

"Oh, no," Les murmured. He turned the ignition key.

"What are you doing, Les?" Dean shouted, looking toward the three girls who were coming their way. "You can't back away from these guys. They're just toying with you!"

"Dean," Charles said, "I wouldn't mess with them or anyone related to them."

THUMP! All three of them spun around and stared out the windshield. Standing over them, his feet planted firmly on the hood of the car, was the driver of the GTO. With a subhuman growl, he drew back the tire iron to strike.

Chapter 15

Les started the engine and threw the Caddy into reverse. The tires shrieked as the car lurched backward.

His bloodshot eyes popping wide open, the GTO driver flew off the car — along with a shower of burgers and fries.

As Les sped away, Dean gazed longingly out the back window. The three girls were following the Caddy with their eyes, looking confused and angry. Leaning against the GTO, the two goons cackled with laughter.

But all of them suddenly backed off when the driver bolted to his feet. His chest pumping wildly, he clenched and unclenched his fists. The veins bulged from his neck as he whipped around and pulled the car door open.

Scurrying like overgrown children, his two friends ran around to the other side of the car and jumped in.

"They're coming after us!" Charles said.

Les pushed the gas pedal to the floor. The GTO jolted backward out of the space — just as another car crossed behind it.

SMACKKK! The GTO came to a dead stop, embedded in the side of the other car. The GTO's driver ripped his door open and climbed out. His face scarlet with rage, he looked back at the damage, then out toward the Cadillac.

Les glanced in his rearview mirror. Archie's was now disappearing behind the trees again.

The Caddy raced into the night. Les steered left and right through the side streets, hoping the GTO wouldn't be able to trace them.

Before long they drove into a desolate factory area. Les looked around desperately for the entrance to the highway. Ahead of them was a fork in the road. Each choice looked like a pathway into limbo.

"Where are we now, Dean?" Charles asked.

Dean held his crumpled piece of paper under the overhead light. "Shoot me. Hang me. What can I say? The directions were for getting there, not for running away!"

Les glided to a stop. "Well, it doesn't really matter at this point, does it?" he snapped. "Which way should we go?"

"Left," said Dean.

"Right," said Charles.

Les shook his head. He veered off to the right and followed the road for a half mile.

Ahead of them, he saw an intersection. A procession of tow trucks snaked across it, moving at a snail's pace.

Civilization, finally, he said to himself.

As the Caddy drew closer to the intersection, the procession continued. Les realized he had to go either left or right; the road didn't continue forward. But the trucks were taking up both lanes. Les came to a full stop.

One tow truck after another crept in front of them, each one pulling a car — first a pickup truck with faded paint, then a Volkswagen Beetle, then a couple of tired-looking old American cars.

"Great, a traffic jam in the middle of the Twilight Zone," Dean said.

"Weird," Charles whispered.

Les put the car in park and waited. He looked down the road for the end of the parade. Suddenly he caught sight of an Audi 5000 Turbo, sticking out like a sore thumb among the older cars as it rolled behind a tow truck.

"That looks like my mother's car," Les remarked.

Just then, off to the right, there was a murmuring of voices. Les looked over. The last tow truck had left, revealing a crowd of people gathered in the middle of the road. A TV crew swarmed around them, accompanied by police cars.

"Here they come!" a couple of voices shouted out.

A cop raised a bullhorn to his mouth and bellowed, "PLEASE DISPERSE THE AREA . . . IMMEDIATELY!"

"What's going on here?" Charles said.

"I don't know," Les answered, "but I'm driving away from them." He shifted to drive and started to turn left.

"You mean, *through* them." Dean said, looking up the road.

Les jammed on the brakes. To the left, heading right toward them, was an enormous object on wheels, covered by a green tarp. It took up the entire width of the street and stretched back farther than they could see. A gleaming metal point stuck out of the tarp.

Les swerved to the right, toward the crowd. The huge thing was behind them now.

"Just keep driving!" Dean shouted. "They'll move aside."

A chant went up from the crowd: "NO NUKES! NO NUKES!"

Les's face turned white. "Th-that . . . that *thing!*" he stammered.

"What? What is it?" Charles said.

"It's . . . it's a Triton missile!" Les said, his voice parched. "That's a demonstration ahead of us! I heard about this on the news!"

"Oh, my . . . " Charles muttered.

"You mean, we could become X-ray images, right before each other's eyes?" Dean said, staring back at the missile with amazement.

"Hang on!" Les said. He screeched to a

stop as the crowd rushed toward them. All around them, hands began slapping the windows. The Caddy began rocking back and forth.

Les hung on to the steering wheel as he looked up into a mob of hostile faces, all unfamiliar to him — except one.

Karl's.

"Hey, I know that guy," Les said. "He's my sister's — "

His eyes bulged as he caught a glimpse of Natalie stalking toward the car. "Oh, pull-eaze!" he exclaimed. "My sister!"

"Where?" Dean asked.

"Duck!" Les shouted. "If she sees us, I'm finished!"

Too late. Natalie stopped by Karl's side and raised her hand to strike the car. But when her eyes met Les's, she froze.

"Please!" Les screamed, looking into her incredulous face. "I beg of you! Don't tell Dad! I'll do anything! I promise!"

"Les! What are you doing?" Natalie wailed. She pulled on Karl's arm, trying to get him to stop. But Karl was lost in his own rage, pounding on the car like a madman.

"Just driving!" Les shrugged his shoulders.

Natalie looked at him in disbelief.

Oh, please don't say it, Les thought. Not in front of my friends. He could see Dean and Charles staring at Natalie, listening to her every word.

"What do you mean, *driving*?" Natalie continued.

No! Les wanted to scream. DON'T SAY IT!

Natalie put her hands on her hips. And at the top of her lungs, she yelled, "You don't even have a license!"

Chapter 16

At least that's what Les assumed she yelled. Her last word was drowned out by an ear-splitting police siren.

As police cars drove up onto the shoulder of the road, the crowd began to thin out. Les inched the car forward past Natalie. There was no way he was going to give her a second chance.

A reporter's voice echoed monotonously through the Andersons' master bedroom:

"As you can see behind me, what started as a peaceful protest against the transportation of five Triton missiles has now mushroomed into a substantial demonstration. . . ."

Behind the reporter, a long, turquoise car crawled across the screen. When it got past a swarm of protesters, it drove away into the distance. But the TV had lingered long enough on its image — there was no mistaking it as Grandpa Anderson's Cadillac. Absolutely everything about it was the same, from the color right on down to the hubcaps.

Or so it would have seemed to Mr. and Mrs. Anderson, if they hadn't been fast asleep.

Les was panicked. He tore down the highway with his foot pressed to the floor.

"I just don't see the big deal," Dean said.

"You don't know my sister, Dean," Les answered. "She's been waiting for this moment her entire life. When I was seven, she woke my parents out of a deep sleep to tell them I swore. I've got to get home."

Dean threw his hands up in desperation. "How is getting home going to change anything? She *saw* you! Does an escaped convict turn himself in when he knows he's going to be executed?"

"If his mother is pregnant and expecting any minute? Yes! There are *no* cars at home. My dad will reinvent the guillotine if he finds out."

The convoy of vehicles carrying the Triton missiles ground to a stop. In front of it, scores of protesters lay on the ground, blocking it from entering town.

Natalie felt her knees give way as Karl dragged her down to the road.

"Natascha, can we please forget the Cadillac and your brother?" he said. "There are far more significant issues in this world."

Natalie shook loose and sat up. "I don't

consider my family an insignificant issue. I've got to get home. With my mother pregnant, and both cars gone, there's no way my father can get to the hospital if he has to."

She stood up and turned to go, until a hand gripped her roughly around the arm. "Karl, let go!" she insisted. She swung around, trying to yank her arm away — and came face-to-face with a policeman.

"Come on, nice and peaceful," the cop said in a gruff voice, pulling her away from the road. Natalie looked to Karl for help but saw him being lifted off the ground by another cop.

She spun back around, and her eyes widened in terror. Ahead of them, dozens of demonstrators were being herded into a paddy wagon. And she and Karl were on their way.

"YOU! PULL OVER! NOW!" A cop with a bullhorn pointed at Les from the shoulder of the road.

"What the — " Les said.

"Do it!" Charles warned. "If you want to spend the night in a room without bars over the windows!"

Les veered onto the shoulder and stopped behind a car with its trunk open. The driver of the car got out and held onto the roof molding to keep from wobbling on his feet. He held out his license to a cop, who examined it under a flashlight.

Les felt himself turning white with fear. "This is great," he said. "This is *really* classic."

"It's only a drunk-driver check," Charles said. "We have nothing to worry about."

"What are you sweating for, Les?" Dean asked. "A license is like a credit card. Sooner or later, you have to break it in."

Les shielded his eyes as a hulking cop leaned into the car and shone a flashlight in his eyes. With a big rush of air, the cop inhaled deeply. He looked suspiciously from Les to Dean to Charles.

Hic!

The three of them looked at each other, panicked. The hiccup was coming from the trunk.

Immediately Dean and Charles shot their hands to their mouths.

"Ooops, sorry," Dean said. "I knew I shouldn't have had those radishes."

Hic!

Les closed his eyes. No, Mercedes, he pleaded inwardly. Don't blow it for me now.

"License and registration," the cop grumbled.

Les couldn't move. He felt paralyzed.

The cop raised his voice. "License and registration, son."

"What's the matter, Les?" Dean said. "Give it to him!"

"I . . . I left my license at home, sir," Les said.

Dean and Charles exchanged a look of amazement.

"Then give me your registration and a piece of I.D."

Les pulled out his wallet and handed the cop his student I.D. card. "This is all I have, sir."

The cop grabbed the card, jotted down the Caddy's plate number, and returned to his car. He reached in through the window to pick up his radio mouthpiece.

Charles looked bewildered. "Why didn't you give him your license, Les?" he asked. "What was that you flashed in front of us before?"

"My school I.D." Les answered sheepishly.

"How could you forget your license your first night out?" Dean said, barely containing a yell.

"I . . . I didn't," Les said. He looked into his friends' eyes. They stared back blankly.

It was now or never, Les thought. He took a deep breath.

"I failed my exam."

"You *what*?" Charles and Dean said at the same time.

"I failed. I got six wrong."

"You mean to tell me you've been driving around all night without a license?" Dean cackled with hysterical laughter.

"At least you did one smart thing tonight," Charles said. "You stole the car from a family member. They're less likely to press charges."

112

Les and Dean turned to each other with a start.

"What's going on?" Charles said.

"We . . . we traded cars," Les said. "With another Caddy from that rent-a-car lot."

Charles looked at Les and Dean as if they were insane. *"You traded cars?* Are you guys lunatics? People go to prison for lesser crimes. We have a future ahead of us! This'll go on our records. We're scarred for life!"

Dean rolled his eyes. "Charles? Will you take a pill or something? We're juveniles. Nothing's going to happen."

"All right, out of there, guys," came the voice of the cop.

The three of them climbed out, and the cop frisked them against the car. "Headquarters tells me you don't have a license, Mr. Anderson," he said.

"W-well, you could say that —" Les stammered.

"Mm-hm. What do you have tied in that trunk? Would you mind opening it for me?"

The *trunk?* Les, Dean, and Charles all gulped at the same time. Les walked to the back of the car, taking small, slow steps. The other two watched him as if he were marching to his death.

Shaking, Les started to open the trunk.

Chapter 17

At that moment, the radio in the cop car crackled to life: *"Emergency four-fifteen riot group, in progress. Maximum assistance is required. . . ."*

The car's siren let out a deafening wail. The cop who was watching Les looked over. His partner leaped out of the car. "Let's go!" he yelled. "We got a four-fifteen at Allied Tech!"

Both cops jumped in the car, and it sped away.

Les still stood at the trunk. He felt numb, on the verge of both laughing and weeping.

"Piece of cake, Les," Dean said, opening the back door of the Caddy. "Let's go get the car."

Sick Sam looked out at his neon sign. The words SICK SAM'S 24-HOUR RENT-A-CAR blazed brightly. Humming to himself, he flicked a switch on the wall. Instantly, the 24-HOUR disappeared. He was ready to go.

He took the cash from the register and stuffed it in a metal box. Then, before he stepped outside, he reached into his desk. Pulling out his revolver, he checked it and put it snugly in his shoulder holster. It was always dangerous to drive around with so much money. You never knew who you might meet.

Silently Les eased his car into a dark spot against the curb. Through the leaves of the nearby trees, he could see the glaring light of Sick Sam's sign — and his grandfather's car, sitting exactly where they'd left it.

He leaned over to Charles. "Now remember, make it sound like you've got a lot of money to spend, but insist on a test drive. Without one, you're not interested. Can you handle that?"

"Do I have a choice?" Charles asked.

Les ignored the question. "Whenever you're ready."

Reluctantly, Charles got out of the car. He gave Les and Dean one last frightened look, turned toward Sick Sam's — and stopped in his tracks.

The Cadillac was slowly backing off the ramp.

"I am dead," Les said. "I am so dead, they're going to have to bury me twice." He jammed the car into gear as Sick Sam squealed out of the lot. "Come on, Charles!"

Charles jumped in, and Les tore away from the curb. Staying a few car lengths away, they followed the Caddy through winding, deserted streets and then onto the highway.

Sick Sam flew down the road at top speed, but Les stayed on his trail. All around them, stretches of barren landscape whooshed by.

Suddenly a blinking light on the dashboard made them all look down. Les felt his stomach sink. "Uh-oh," he said. "The gas guage."

"Why couldn't you have stolen a Honda or a diesel Rabbit," Charles moaned, a whimper in his voice, "something with better highway mileage?"

"Charles, I know it's uncomfortable sitting in wet diapers, but can you just quit crying for a minute?" Dean shot back. Then he turned to Les. "I'd say at the most you have thirty miles in the reserve tank. At the least, you have ten."

Les pressed the trip-mileage indicator so that it read zero.

When Sick Sam finally turned onto an exit ramp, the indicator read nine. Les kept behind him.

The car jounced over potholes as Sick Sam led them through narrow, neglected streets. Hollow shells of houses stood beside rubble-strewn lots. Trash littered the sidewalks, and discarded newspapers floated along in the breeze like tumbleweeds.

Charles gulped. "I've never seen this neighborhood."

"I think it's a testing site for those Triton missiles," Dean said.

Les tried to laugh, but he couldn't. Not here. Not in a very shiny, very valuable car.

The farther away from the highway they drove, the worse the neighborhood became. Les glanced at the indicator, which now read twelve.

"Les! Slow down!" Dean whispered, pointing ahead.

Les eased his foot onto the brake. Ahead of them, Sick Sam was turning into a dark alley. Les cut off his lights and crept up just to the edge of the alley.

They all craned their necks to see around the corner. At the end of the alley, Sick Sam parked in front of the only building that seemed to have any life in it.

It just wasn't clear what kind of life it was. An ancient neon BAR sign hung lopsided in front, and roaring, animal-like noises floated into the street from within.

"I've heard of being hard-up for a drink," Dean said, "but this is ridiculous."

Charles looked pale. "I don't think I'd want to go in there."

"I don't think the Terminator would want to go in there," Les replied.

As the three of them tried to plot a strategy, Sick Sam turned off the lights and the ignition. He casually checked the gun in his holster, then slipped his cash box under the dashboard on the passenger side.

Making sure to lock up, he lumbered into the bar.

Les waited until Sick Sam was inside, then said to Dean, "As soon as you see me turn the lights on, pull in behind me. And leave his key in the ignition. It's the least we can do."

"Are you sure the hide-a-key is still in the car?" Charles asked.

"It'd better be there," Les answered. He turned back to Dean. "Are you ready?"

Dean's eyes sparkled. "Les, I was *born* ready."

Les got out of the car and sprinted down the alley. He knelt down behind his grandfather's Caddy and felt around underneath the rear bumper for the hide-a-key. It wasn't there. He ran around to the front bumper.

And as he reached under it, the sudden blare of a car horn made every muscle tighten.

The horn sounded like a funeral march.

Les threw himself under the Caddy, lying flat on his back. He found himself staring right at the hide-a-key box. Opening it, he grabbed the key.

The low rumble of an engine got louder. Les could see a set of four chrome wheels roll up beside him.

A familiar gravelly voice said, "Hey, that's

the Caddy that messed us up. Let's trash it, man!"

Les felt sick as he watched three pairs of filthy boots clomp onto the ground beside him — along with the tip of the tire iron and the metal head of a sledgehammer.

His mind raced. What could he do now? If he didn't die now, his father would kill him later anyway. He'd managed to get through the night so far without harming the car at all. There was no *way* he could let anything happen to it —

CRASSSSSSH! WHOMMP! THWACKK!

Les felt the car shudder as shards of glass showered onto the ground.

Or maybe it wasn't the car. Maybe the shudder was from Les's own body. It was hard to tell. Especially with his life speeding before his eyes like a video on fast-forward.

Chapter 18

Les cringed with each blow. He couldn't take it any more.

Finally something in his mind snapped. He grabbed onto the Caddy's tailpipe and pushed himself out from under the car. "Hey! Hey!" he yelled. "What do you think you're doing, man?"

The three goons stared at him, slack-jawed. Les checked out the car. The headlights had been kicked in. The windshield wipers, side mirrors, and hubcaps lay mangled on the ground. He spun around and held out his hand to the driver. "Give me that sledge-hammer!"

Stunned, the driver didn't move.

Les looked at him as if he were a mis-behaving child. "Come on! What are you, attached to it? Give me it!" He lunged forward and grabbed the hammer out of the driver's hand. "You think you geniuses know how to wreck a car? *I'll* show you turkeys how to wreck a car!"

Les held the sledgehammer over his head, looked up toward the heavens with a prayer, and brought it down on the front bumper.

To everyone's surprise, the bumper crashed to the ground with a dull *clonk*.

Les turned back around confidently. "*That's* how you wreck a car. None of this sissy side-mirror stuff. My grandmother could knock that off with a walking stick." He casually tossed the sledgehammer back to the driver. "Here's your teddy bear."

Les's speech was met by eyes that grew meaner by the second. "Now," he continued, "I'm gonna walk inside this stinkhole, plant my body down at the bar, and get messed up. And when I walk outta there in twenty minutes, you Popsicle-licking wimps better not be playing with my ride." He pointed to the GTO. "Otherwise I'm gonna have to show you dudes how a one-man wrecking crew acts when he feels like throwing a party."

Stupefied, Charles and Dean watched as Les walked into the bar, followed close behind by the three angry goons.

"Come on," Dean said, reaching for the door handle. "We have to do something."

The two of them slipped out of the Caddy and ran toward the bar.

* * *

With a swagger that was meant to be like John Wayne but looked more like Pee-Wee Herman, Les walked up to the door of the bar and kicked it open.

He found himself staring into a sea of bloodshot eyes, ripped T-shirts, and tattooed biceps. There was grime on the walls and ceilings. There was grime where the paint had peeled away. In this place, even the grime had grime.

As the door crashed against the wall, everything immediately stopped — the music, the people, even the rats. Nestled in the back, Sick Sam sat with a woman who made the bride of Frankenstein look like a cover girl.

Les rocked from side to side as he sauntered to the bar. The floorboards creaked beneath his Nikes. All eyes followed him. Simmering anger hung so thick in the air that even the three goons stayed back by the door.

Growling like confused jungle beasts, two burly guys pulled their girlfriends aside and made room for Les at the bar. A layer of grease coated the bar top, but Les leaned over it to come eye-to-eye with a snarling bartender.

"We just ran out of Kool-Aid," the bartender grumbled.

Les chuckled coolly. "Bourbon," he said. "Straight up."

As the bartender poured a shot glass full

of bourbon, Les glanced around him. All eyes were still fixed on him. Not one person had moved since he came in. Through the window, he could see Charles and Dean, looking as if they were about to see their best friend thrown to the lions.

Les turned back to the bar. He picked up the overflowing shot glass. A voice inside him reminded him that he'd never had a drink in his life. He ignored the voice and inhaled the drink.

The liquor caught in his mouth. It felt as if he had just tasted Drano. He felt his eyes bug out. This was the moment of truth. . . .

With a grimace of contempt, he spat the bourbon across the bar. Then, before anyone could react, he thrust his face to within an inch of the bartender's. "I thought you said you ran out of Kool-Aid," he said. The bartender stared back at him, bewildered. "How 'bout something with a little body — something with some heat in it!"

His lips curling into a sinister smile, the bartender reached under the bar and pulled out a musty bottle of the nastiest-looking liquid Les had ever seen. There was no label on the bottle, but resting at the bottom of it was a bloated, brown worm.

The bartender poured Les a glass. By now, the crowd had begun to stir — including the three goons. They all gathered around Les to watch.

Sweat beaded on Les's forehead. Come on, keep it up, he said to himself. If you blow it, you're history.

With a cool swipe of his hand, he pushed the glass aside — and grabbed the bottle! All around him, the crowd gasped. Les turned the bottle upside down and let it pour out into the palm of his hand. The liquor splashed through his fingers onto the bar, until he was left holding the worm in the palm of his hand.

He held the worm firmly between his thumb and index finger and lifted it for all to see. Then, with a dramatic gesture, he threw his head back, dropped the worm into his mouth, and swallowed.

A roar of approval burst out in the bar. Within seconds the music came back on and the place returned to normal. The two Neanderthal-types behind Les grinned and turned back to their girlfriends.

Les looked around proudly — and found himself staring into the torsos of the three goons from the GTO.

"Step outside, *worm*," the driver said menacingly. "We've got a job to finish."

Les looked around for support. But his new friends were wrapped up in their own snarling conversations. They seemed to have forgotten him already.

Behind him, one of the Neanderthal-types put his beer on the bar. In a fit of inspiration, Les reached back and grabbed the beer.

Pushing the GTO driver away from him, he said, "Back off, man! Don't crowd me!"

The driver had murder in his eyes. His muscles tensed as he took a step toward Les. "Why you —"

In a flash, Les whipped the beer over his shoulder, drenching the guy he had taken it from. Then he tossed the empty glass at the driver, who caught it instinctively.

Quickly Les stepped aside. The beastlike guy at the bar bellowed and turned around — to come face-to-face with the GTO driver, holding the empty glass.

As the goons stood in shock, the guy uncorked a haymaker to the driver's jaw, sending him flying across a table.

And as Les scurried toward the front door, the words "BARRRR FIIIIGHT!" rang out like a war cry above the raucous din.

Chapter 19

"Quick!" Les yelled as he burst out the door.
"Switch!"

Les jumped into his grandfather's car and
squealed away from the curb, sending the discarded metal junk flying.

Charles and Dean scrambled back up the
street. They hopped into Sick Sam's Caddy
and shot into the space that Les had just
cleared. As Les waited up the road, they
frantically opened the back door and pulled
out the golf clubs and the cooler.

Running as fast as they could, they lugged
the stuff to the other Caddy, tossed it inside,
and dove in.

Les left skid marks in the road as he barreled away.

"HOOOO-HOO! HAAAAA!" All three of
them exploded with laughter as they put
distance between themselves and the bar.

Sitting in the passenger seat, Dean clapped
his hands and stomped his feet wildly.

Clank. Dean's foot came down on a beat-up old metal cash box. "What's this?" he said.

Before anyone could answer, Les stamped on the brakes. Dean pitched forward into the dashboard. "Hey! What are you doing?" he yelled.

A look of blind panic in his eyes, Les shoved the car into reverse. "Mercedes!" he said.

Charles and Dean bolted upright. In unison they cried out, "Ohhhh, no!"

Les turned around. Sam's Cadillac was now a few blocks away. He stepped on the accelerator. The car hurtled backward, pitching from side to side.

He stopped right beside the other car. The doors swung open, and the three of them flew into action. Charles dumped the cash box into Sam's backseat. Dean ran and opened the trunk.

Slowly, carefully, Les lifted Mercedes out of the trunk. She opened her eyes and wrapped her arms around him in a shaky embrace. Les put her into the backseat of his Caddy. He took one last look at the bar — and felt his blood turn to ice.

Staring back at him through the smeared window, his mouth hanging open, was Sick Sam!

The three of them flung themselves into the car, and Les rocketed down the street.

"We did it!" Charles yelled, bouncing up and down. "Man, we did it!"

Dean clapped Les on the shoulder. "Awesome, Les! That was hall-of-fame material!"

CRRACCCKK! . . . *SMASSHHH!* Les swerved as the back window exploded into a million pieces. His eyes wide with fear, he looked into his rearview mirror.

Framed by the shattered glass, Sick Sam was standing by the bar, leveling his gun for a second shot.

The right side of the Caddy practically lifted off the road as Les veered onto a side street. His rear tires jumped the curb, plowing the back of the car into a lamppost. With a sickening metallic clank, the bumper tore off and clattered to the ground.

The neighborhood rushed by them as Les's speedometer strained past seventy miles an hour. He looked back into his mirror. Sam was nowhere to be seen.

Charles and Dean sat peering out the back window, their bodies hunched in fearful anticipation.

Just then an unexpected voice broke the tense silence. "Oooh, what happened?"

Next to Dean, Mercedes had begun to stir. Her eyes blinked open. "I . . . I'm sorry. I must have dozed off."

With a broad grin, Dean stuck his face two inches away from hers and said, "You didn't miss a *thing*!"

Mercedes closed her eyes again. And like three hyenas let out of a cage, Les, Dean, and Charles screamed with laughter.

* * *

Back at the bar, Sick Sam angrily pulled open the door of his Cadillac. His face was twisted with vengeance as he turned to climb in.

But out of the corner of his eye, he caught sight of the cash box. He lifted it. It was still heavy with money. He tried to open it, but it was locked tight. Just the way he'd left it.

I must have come out just in time, he thought. With a shrug, he headed back into the bar.

At the county jail that night, the halls echoed with singing.

"Where have all . . . the flowers gone. . . ."

Natalie sat alone in a corner, morose. In the center of the holding cell, Karl was sitting cross-legged with a group of protesters. They were all holding hands and swaying back and forth.

Another time, she would have been right in there with them, but not now. Not when her mother faced the possibility of being the first woman in Sunny Meadows to have to *walk* to the hospital while in labor!

"When will they ever learn? . . . When will they ever learn?"

The lyrics made her think of her brother and his friends. It was a good question — when *would* they ever learn?

Come to think of it, she said to herself as

she looked at Karl, when will *I* ever learn? It's just as much my fault!

She folded her arms and stared out the barred window. The sun was beginning to creep over the horizon. Oh, well, maybe the baby will hold off until we all get home.

At the same time, a gasp interrupted the silence in the Andersons' bedroom. Mrs. Anderson sat up sharply. She grabbed her stomach and moaned. Easy now, she thought. It's not serious until the contractions are less than four minutes apart.

She looked at her watch, then at her sleeping husband.

Precisely three minutes later, an excruciating pain shot through her.

The only thought running through her mind was the hope that the cars were filled with gas.

Chapter 20

By the time Les found his way to Dean's street, the houses and trees were glowing with the strange silver-gray light of dawn. The battered Cadillac glided to a stop in front of Dean's house.

Charles and Dean slipped quietly out of the car. They closed the door gently, taking care not to wake up Mercedes.

Dean leaned into the car with a wide smile. "License or no license, Les," he said, "that was one intense display of driving."

Charles nodded. "You could be the only sixteen-year-old in the country to open a stunt-driving school without a license."

"You really set the standard for a first night out with the car," Dean said. "It's gonna be a tough one to top."

Les laughed. "Luckily *you* don't get *your* license for a few months."

"What are you going to tell Sleeping

Beauty?" Dean asked, looking back at Mercedes.

"I don't know," Les said with a shrug. "I may not tell her anything. . . ."

Mercedes let out a groan and shifted positions. Putting his finger to his mouth, Les signaled Dean and Charles to be quiet.

Les waved to his friends as he drove down the street. Their faces were wide-eyed and smiling, as if they'd had some sort of religious experience.

It was easy enough for *them* to feel that way, Les thought. To them, it was all over.

But Les had a creeping sensation of doom. What began as an innocent drive had exploded in his face. Now here he was at dawn, without a license, with an unconscious girl and a bottle of vodka in the backseat, in his grandfather's car that he'd stolen and then ruined. . . . He knew his troubles were far from over.

As the first rays of the sun peeked through the trees, Les pulled up to Mercedes's house. He opened the rear door and gently lifted her out of the car.

"Oh, Les!" Mercedes cried as she awakened from her sleep. She looked up groggily into his eyes. "I . . . I just had the most bizarre dream! It was as if I were . . . *trapped* inside the trunk of a car! And then suddenly the trunk flipped open and there you were, rescuing me. It was so weird!"

Les carried her up the path to her front

door. He tried to laugh nonchalantly. "It, uh, *does* sound kind of crazy. . . ."

"Oh, I know it does. But somehow you were always there, Les — to hold me, like you are right now. I felt so safe and. . . ." She reached up and caressed his cheek. ". . . and so warm."

Les opened his mouth to speak, but he couldn't. He had so much he wanted to say — about what had really happened that night, about the way she tore him apart just by looking at him — but his feelings were all bottled up inside of him. It felt like . . . like gridlock of the soul, he thought.

Mercedes looked at Les sheepishly as he set her down at the doorstep. "I'm sorry I was such a sleepyhead tonight," she said. "You must have been so bored."

"Don't be silly," Les answered with a smile. "For me it was nonstop action."

"Les?" Mercedes said softly, moving closer to him. "When can we go out again?"

"Well, right now would be great, actually. Tonight may be the last time anyone sees me."

"Why? What happened?"

Les shook his head. "It's a long, complicated story. I'm sure you don't want to hear it."

Mercedes gave him a coy smile. "Does it have a happy ending?"

"It has so far," Les said, beaming. "Maybe one day I'll get to tell you how it ends . . . if I live."

"Well. . . ." Mercedes nestled up close to him. "I'll be waiting, Les."

Mercedes gazed up at him with eyes like deep blue pools. Slowly she brought her lips close to his. And all the tension, all the intimidation Les had been feeling melted away in a tender, passionate kiss.

Mrs. Anderson's chest heaved as she gasped for breath. She leaned over and shook her husband. "Robert!"

"Mmmmm," Mr. Anderson mumbled.

"Robert, wake up! This is it!"

Mr. Anderson shifted sleepily. "Right, honey . . . go back to — " Suddenly he threw back the covers. "This is *it*? Did you say this is it?"

Mrs. Anderson nodded. She clutched her stomach in pain.

"Okay, short breaths. Short breaths," Mr. Anderson said, demonstrating. He grabbed a shirt and a pair of pants out of his closet and put them on as Mrs. Anderson sat up at the edge of the bed.

"Please, Robert, let's go now!"

"We're on our way, dear," Mr. Anderson said, struggling with his shoes. "We're on our way."

And before he bent down to help her outside, he reached over to his night table and grabbed the keys to Grandpa Anderson's Cadillac.

* * *

Les waited patiently at the red light. It seemed ridiculous to sit there at a full stop at five in the morning, with no one awake within miles. Les crept forward, but then stopped. At this point, he didn't think he could afford to break any more laws. Why not just wait a few more seconds?

He sat tapping the steering wheel, looking around at the birds fluttering from tree to tree, whistling to himself. . . .

Mr. Anderson clutched the banister as he helped his wife down the stairs. "Relax," he said, "Just try to breathe naturally."

"Ohhhhh," Mrs. Anderson moaned, reaching for a chair. "Nothing about this is natural."

"Come on. We'll be in the car in two seconds." Mr. Anderson carefully led her out the back door. He looked at the garage. All he had to do was walk her a few more feet.

With each step, Mrs. Anderson gritted her teeth. Her pained, squinting eyes were focused on the garage door.

"One more second," her husband said. "We're almost there!"

With one arm around her, he reached for the handle of the garage door — and swung it open.

Chapter 21

Les edged up the driveway. He felt his body go numb all over. He couldn't have *picked* a worse time to come home. In front of him, his father was opening the garage door, while his mother held her stomach in pain.

This is it, Les thought. I'm disowned as of today. They probably won't even let me see the baby. But just as the door began to rise, Les saw his mother put out her hand and say something. Les's dad turned to face her, letting go of the door. His back was to it as it swung open, revealing the empty space within. He seemed totally wrapped up in Les's mom.

Holding his breath, praying against all hope that they wouldn't see him, Les cruised into the open garage.

"What do you mean, you're okay?" Mr. Anderson said to his wife, his eyes wild with confusion.

Mrs. Anderson breathed in and out calmly, as if testing to see if there was any pain. "It must have been gas," she said. "False alarm. I feel fine now. I'm sorry, Robert."

"Are you *sure* you don't want to go to the hospital, honey? The car's right here."

He held his hand out to the garage. Out of the corner of his eye, he could make out the dark outline of Grandpa Anderson's Cadillac, enveloped in the shadows of the garage.

"I'm positive," Mrs. Anderson replied, with a guilty look. "It . . . it must have been the herring."

Mr. Anderson nodded, then reached up to the door. But just as he was about to pull it down, he stopped short.

"What's the matter?" his wife asked.

"Why was the garage door unlocked?"

"I don't know. Maybe Natalie left it open?"

"Why would she? She took the Audi."

His brow furrowed, Mr. Anderson walked out to the front of the house. He bristled with anger when he saw the Audi wasn't back.

Then he looked at the front lawn — and his mouth dropped open in shock. Like two deep wounds, a set of tracks had been gouged across his freshly cut grass.

"Robert!"

He stared at the lawn, as if in a trance. His wife's voice didn't even register.

"Robert!"

Finally he snapped out of it. Spinning

around, he saw her hunched over in pain. He ran back and propped her up.

"Okay, honey," he said, walking her into the garage. "We're going to the hospital right now. Just try to breathe — "

Suddenly he stopped. Everything went blank — his wife, the garage, the world around him — everything except for the battered hulk in front of him.

He circled around the car, gaping at the damage. He put his hand through the hole that used to be the rear window. Each mutilated part of the car felt like a punch in the stomach — the missing bumpers, the severed mirrors, the mangled wipers.

He looked into the car, and caught sight of his son huddled on the floor, shaking. Red-and-white specks began to cloud his vision. He felt his upper lip rise above his teeth.

"Is there something wrong with your bed, Les?" he said, his voice a rasp.

Les slithered out the opposite door. Neither of them seemed to notice Mrs. Anderson, doubled over against the side of the car.

"Would you mind telling me what size shark was responsible for this?" Mr. Anderson said.

Les gulped. "I . . . uh. . . ."

"No. I don't want to know. Save it for the judge." His eyes blazed. "Do you have any notion of what you've done this evening? What this means to your future in this house and on this planet?"

"I have a feeling," Les said.

"Les, you couldn't even begin to imagine what's in store for you. We had a college fund set aside for you. That's gone. You had free room and board, two trusting parents, and a social life. *That's* gone. You had a TV, a stereo, a baseball glove, a tennis racket, a skateboard, a bicycle — even sunlight and a window in your room. That's all gone. I'm boarding up the window tomorrow. And communication with the outside world? You can forget about it! It's all history. Frankly, Les, I don't see what's left . . . other than school and two bus rides a day."

"Robert. . . ." Mrs. Anderson cried out weakly.

"And don't even *think* about a license," Les's dad went on.

"Never?" Les said.

"Les, as long as I'm alive and you and I share the same last name, you will never, *not ever*, sit behind a steering wheel — except in your dreams." By now he was breathing so hard his nostrils flared. "All I can say, buddy boy, is that you are *damn* lucky your mother didn't go into labor tonight."

"Robert!" Mrs. Anderson pleaded. "I *am* in labor."

Mr. Anderson crash-landed back to reality. "Are you sure?"

"Yes!"

Running around the car, Les's dad circled one arm around her and opened the back door with his other arm. He lowered her gently into the seat, then began to close the door.

Mrs. Anderson grabbed the door handle. "No, stay here. I want you to be with me."

"In the backseat? Who's going to drive?"

Mrs. Anderson raised her head. Her face was etched with pain. With desperate, pleading eyes, she looked at her oldest son.

"Les can."

Chapter 22

Les felt like a dying animal being eyed by a vulture. He tried to smile.

"Les?" Mr. Anderson bellowed. "Les who? Not *this* Les! No way! Les is staying here." He turned his head back to the house. "RUDYYYYY."

Rudy, who had been waiting at the back door in his pajamas, came scampering outside.

"Rudy, get in the back with your mom!" Mr. Anderson ordered.

"Robert, please!" Mrs. Anderson protested. "It's been nine months. That's long enough. Let's go!"

Mr. Anderson looked at his wife, then at Les. His eyes were still on fire.

But Les's fear had lifted. The first thing on his mind was his mother. He couldn't bear to see her in such pain.

He had to do something about it, even if it seemed futile. "Dad, I know I let you down," he said. "And I'm as sorry as I can ever be that I disappointed you. But as hard as you try, you can't imagine what I've learned tonight." He looked straight into his father's eyes. "Please let me drive, Dad. I can do it."

Mr. Anderson exhaled. He narrowed his eyes and leaned in close to his son's face. "All right," he said, putting the keys in Les's hand. "But try to drive like you have a license."

Les grinned as his dad and Rudy hopped in. Settling behind the driver's seat, he backed out of the driveway.

Natalie hung up the phone. Her worst fear had come true. No one was at her house.

Karl's face was glowing with energy. "Don't you feel invigorated?" he said. "This is just the beginning. There are many wars still to wage. You and I, Natascha. Together we will bring the running-dog imperialists to their knees."

Natalie whipped around. She had heard that line a million times. Suddenly it sounded so ridiculous. It was one thing to be concerned about protecting the world from nuclear weapons, but it was another thing to be lost in a fanatical dream. "Buzz off, Karl!" she blurted out. She turned to the front door, where a policeman was releasing the protesters from the station house. "And by the way, the name is *Natalie*, not Natascha!"

Holding her chin up, she walked out the door.

For the first time since she'd met him, Karl was speechless.

Les stomped on the brake. Everyone in the car lunged forward. His mother groaned with pain. The Caddy left a long skid as it squealed to a stop.

"Les, what are you doing? There's not a car in sight!" Mr. Anderson said.

Les pointed upward. "It's a red light."

"We're rushing your mother to the hospital, not to a bridge game! Go through it! Just get us there!"

Les looked both ways, then pressed the accelerator.

RRRRROOOOOOOMMMM! The engine revved, but they weren't moving.

"I don't believe this!" Mr. Anderson said. "Sounds like the transmission blew." He leaned over to the front. "Try the other gears."

Les shifted into neutral, then into low gear. The car stayed put.

Frustrated, he shifted into park, passing through reverse. The car jolted backward.

"Only reverse works," he said.

"Oooooh!" Mrs. Anderson cried out.

Les looked at his dad, shrugging his shoulders.

Mr. Anderson winced sympathetically

along with his wife's pain. He nodded to Les. "All right, go for it. But take it easy."

With a big smile, Les did a U-turn in reverse. Bracing his arm on the back of his seat, he fixed his eyes out the back window and peeled off.

The car bombed down the street backward, wavering from side to side. In the left lane, a long wedding procession snaked along.

"Make a right at the next street!" Mr. Anderson said. Then he realized he was facing the wrong way. "I mean a left! You know what I mean!"

What he meant was that Les had to get across the wedding procession somehow. Les stepped on the gas, zipping past the baffled glances of the passengers in the other cars. The first car was just about at the intersection.

But it pitched forward in a sudden stop as Les cut it off.

Brakes shrieked and horns blared as Les made a left turn onto a city street — just as a blind woman crossed into his pathway!

With a sudden yank of the steering wheel, Les jumped the sidewalk, missing her by inches. He barreled headlong into a crowd of empty restaurant tables set up for outdoor brunch. Holding a red tablecloth, a waiter dove out of the way like a matador teasing a bull. The Caddy flew through the tablecloth and kept going.

144

RREEEEEOOOOOO! A siren cut through the morning air.

Les steered back onto the street, weaving in and out of the traffic lanes, followed close behind by a motorcycle cop.

"SHE'S PREGNANT!" Mr. Anderson roared to the cop.

Before Les knew it, he could see the motorcycle racing up beside him. The cop leaned into the window. "FOLLOW M — " he started to say.

The next moment, he wasn't there. Les glanced over to see him flying through the air over the top of an antique convertible. His motorcycle was still standing, smashed against the car's rear bumper.

The cop landed in the front seat next to the driver, a red-faced guy with a hip flask. The man did a double take at the cop, smiled, and took another swig.

Les bulleted down the street. The hospital was in sight, just beyond the next intersection.

Les's eyes strained in all directions. A construction site jutted out into the street just beyond the intersection. Across from it was a police station.

And in front of them, a flood overflowed into the street. Les's mind raced back to his driver's test, to his experience earlier that night. His foot froze. Above them, the light had turned yellow. Cars on either side of the intersection began to inch forward.

Just as the light turned to red, Les lifted his foot off the accelerator. The Cadillac sliced through the water like a cabin cruiser, spraying the sidewalk.

Mr. Anderson shielded his wife as water gushed into the car, soaking them. His eyes were wide with fear. In the front seat, Rudy bounced up and down, squealing with laughter.

Les exhaled as he passed through safely. He focused on the hospital — or tried to. A familiar figure was walking out of the police precinct, staring goggle-eyed at him.

Glancing quickly over, he saw it was only Natalie. He turned back to face the road.

Natalie? What's she doing there? he thought. His eyes darted over to her again.

"LOOK OOOOUUUUT!" Mr. Anderson bellowed.

Les looked back to the street — just in time to see a towering crane from the construction site swinging a set of heavy steel girders right into their path.

With inches to spare, Les swooped around them and right up to the front of the hospital.

Natalie rushed up to the car and pulled the door open. Immediately two orderlies dashed out of the hospital with a wheelchair. Mr. Anderson lifted his wife out of the backseat and into one of the chairs.

Les got out as the others rushed Mrs. Anderson toward the hospital door. He felt anchored to the car. A wave of shame ran through him as he looked at it. If he hadn't been so greedy, if he hadn't felt like he had to impress Mercedes, this would have been so much easier. He wouldn't have put everyone's life in danger — including a new brother or sister who wasn't even born yet.

And he wouldn't have ruined his grandfather's prized possession.

"Les, come here!" he heard his father say.

He looked up. His dad was standing alone by the hospital door, a stern look on his face.

Les's feet shuffled along the ground as he skulked over, slump-shouldered.

Mr. Anderson reached out and put his arm around him. "Where did you learn to drive like that?" he said, amazed.

Les felt a huge weight lift from his shoulders. His dad was actually smiling! "I don't know, Dad. I guess last night."

"It must have been some crash course."

Les laughed as his dad gave him an affectionate squeeze. "What about the car?" Les said.

Mr. Anderson shrugged. "Maybe we can fix the car before Grandpa gets home. He'll never notice."

Les's face broke out into a broad smile. Together, he and his dad walked into the hospital.

The Cadillac sat outside, pinging slightly as its engine rested from the long night. If it were a person, it would have crawled into the hospital for treatment.

Maybe not. Instead, it may have looked up and seen the enormous girders hovering over it, teetering at the end of a wobbly crane. In panic, it may have torn out into the street when it saw the construction workers shouting and running for cover.

But it wasn't a person. In fact, before two seconds were up, it wasn't much of a car, either. With a deafening *BOOOOOOM*, the girders crashed down on top of it.

And when the cloud of dust began to settle, when the last piece of chrome tinkled to the ground, a voice floated up from among the scraps. It sounded like Frank Sinatra, and it came from the only moving thing in the rubble — a creaking cassette player. But as it echoed in the morning air, it may as well have been the voice of the car itself:

"That's life. . . ."